CLOUDED

BY

ENVY

CANDACE ROBINSON

Copyright © 2020 by Candace Robinson
Cover Design by Hannah-Sternjakob-Design
Edited by Live Knudsen and Jackie Turner

This is a work of fiction. Names, characters, places and incidents either are the product of the author's imagination or are used fictitiously, and any resemblance to any actual persons, living or dead, events, or locales is entirely coincidental. This book may not be used or reproduced in any manner without written permission from the author.

For those who have experienced a bit of
envy

One

Brenik
Ten Years Ago

Brenik could not get the vision of the headless sarillas' bodies he had seen yesterday out of his head. Their necks looked to be perfectly snapped but when he had inched closer, he could see the outline of where the skin had been ripped, blood leaking onto their dark fur. The jovkins had only eaten the heads, and the sarillas' torn bodies were left to rest in the damp grass, as if at peace.

Shaking the vision out of his thoughts, Brenik stood on a tree branch beside his sister, Brayora. He studied the creature in front of them, Junah, and listened intently to what she needed to say.

"You two must flee while you are still able—before there is nowhere for you to hide any longer," Junah said with sweat beading against her temples.

The long black horns sprouting from her forehead appeared to penetrate into Brenik's thoughts, while the shorter ones attached to her temples pointed in two different directions, as if confusing him in which way he should flee.

Brayora lunged forward and flew down to wrap her arms

around Junah's thick ankle. "Junah, we do not want to run and hide away again. You have been like a mother to us this whole time, and what if something happens to Brenik? I… I would not be able to live with myself!" she cried as her tearstained face turned toward Brenik.

He wanted Bray to be free from harm, but more than anything, he wanted himself to remain safe. Turning her head back around, Bray buried her face flat against Junah's leg. Brenik watched as Bray's black braid fluttered against her obsidian wings—each thin vein seemed to pulse rapidly with the fright of having to leave their home. Bray gently lifted her head, released Junah's ankle, and took several steps back.

Brenik dove off from the branch, beating his wings until his bare feet hit the cool grass beside his sister. If not for their dark wings, sharper teeth, and pointier ears, he and Bray could easily be mistaken for fairies.

Junah's giant form knelt in front of them. She stared down at Brenik and Bray intently, her golden eyes beaming against her gray skin. Keeping silent, they waited for Junah to speak.

"I am going to let you two little ones know a secret I once attempted myself. It did not work for me, but it may for you. I did not want it to come down to this, but sometimes things do not work out the way we would like." She paused for a moment before speaking again, and worry coursed through Brenik's small body. "Away from here—about half a day's journey to the south—you will stumble upon an ivory, rose-shaped stone. Once there, place your hand against the petals and wait for the Stone of Desire to rise, then you may ask for safe crossing. If worthy, you shall pass. If not, you will have to continue hiding. The jovkins have started to hunt the sarillas more and more, but bats are still their priority."

Brenik knew Junah was right—the fact that they were bats made them vulnerable. Their race had been long hunted in Laith by the jovkins—Junah's kind. The jovkins claimed the bats ate all their fruits, but Brenik's race was so tiny in comparison to them that it should not have mattered. But what was theirs was theirs, the jovkins seemed to think.

Reaching desperately for Bray's dry hand, Brenik clenched it with his sweat-slicked one. It irked him that she was not as frightened as him.

Pulling him closer, Bray leaned her head as far back as she could to gaze up at Junah. "I will do whatever I can to protect my brother." The tears that had streamed down Bray's cheeks were already dried, but against her pale skin, her red lips still resembled the color of blood from her sobbing.

When Brenik and Brayora were born, their mother left them behind because there were two of them. Usually, only one bat was born at a time—but there were two who drew their first breath that day. Brenik was too insignificant for his mother to worry about, and because Bray had gotten most of the nourishment—she had been perfectly healthy. It was always her fault. Junah had found Bray and Brenik near a peach tree— instead of destroying their fragile bodies as she was meant to have done, she had taken care of them ever since.

Laying a large open hand against the luscious grass, Junah gave them both a tilt of the head. Brenik and Bray stepped forward onto her palm, and she brought them both up to her shoulder. Bray was the first to step from Junah's large hand, and she lunged for the jovkin's neck in a long hug, arms unable to even wrap halfway around her. Brenik stood on the end of Junah's shoulder and watched as she mumbled to Bray that she loved her. With one last kiss to the neck, Bray fluttered off, allowing Brenik to finally say his goodbye.

Rushing forward to the warmth of Junah's gray neck, he wrapped his thin arms around her as much as they would go— which wasn't far. "I will miss you, Junah," he said as tiny tears dribbled down his cheeks.

Junah's neck creaked as she turned to face him, and he backed away to the edge of her shoulder. She appeared tired, and her age was beginning to show—in the deep lines across her forehead and the wrinkles that sketched beside her eyes. "Brenik, there is a darkness and jealousy in you which has to stop now. I know you love your sister, but the envy needs to cease, or it will destroy everything that is a part of you. I have seen your kindness, Brenik. You both mean everything to me, so protect each other because I love you."

With a sharp inhale, he leaped from Junah's shoulder. Brenik thought about the words the jovkin had spoken and although he cared about her deeply, he could not mutter those words back.

A loud howl traveled through the forest, followed by an ear-piercing scream of agony. Brenik flinched midair because he always recognized the sound of a jovkin tearing its victim to pieces.

"Go!" Junah hissed.

Not turning back once to look at Junah, he flapped his dark wings fiercely, until he found Bray at the edge of the forest, standing on a small branch with black leaves.

"We have to hurry, little brother. It will be all right," she murmured, as if she were in charge and the only one who was okay. Well, *he* was okay, too.

Choosing not to answer his sister, Brenik zoomed right past her. *How dare she always call me little brother?* he thought. It was only because she was born before him by barely any wing beats. A trickle of laughter came from behind him as they soared through the air, like he was playing a game with her. At her sounds, a smile crossed his face because maybe he was.

Brenik's wings pumped quicker and quicker as he flew past more inky leaves. The foliage changed colors as he flew farther—to sapphire, followed by a deep pink. Hearing her inch closer, he tried to flap even faster, but she was too swift. Bray gave him a small wink when she caught up, then whipped her head forward and zipped by.

There was no sign of sweat on her face, while Brenik was soaked in perspiration. Wet beads pressed to the back of his shirt, making the material of his tunic cling heavily against his skin and slow him down.

Sighing, Brenik wanted to give up. There was nothing he was better at than her. Always second best. Always nothing. He loved her… He hated her… But he needed her because he would miss her more than anything.

"Wait, Bray!" he yelled, not wanting to be left behind by himself.

Spinning around, she gave him a playful grin until she saw his face. "What is wrong, Brenik?"

"Just… Just... Don't leave me behind. Please," he stuttered, hating himself even more for the weakness of needing her.

They both came to a halt for a moment on a large crooked branch.

"I would never leave you behind," Bray said. "I love you, and I am always here to protect you. Always have been—always will be." She wrapped her arms tightly around his back, and tugged him into a solid hug.

Pausing for a moment with his hands at his sides, Brenik finally brought them up to hold her just as tight. She was his only family now. When they were first born, right before they could fly, Bray had attempted with all her might to carry him because he was not strong enough to move his wings. She helped him get through it, yet it was also her fault that he was the way he was—even though it was not.

Brenik pushed the conflicting thoughts away. "I am here for you, too," he said. They had only been alive in Laith for ten years, but after all they had been through, it felt much longer than that.

Slowly releasing him, Bray dove from the tree. Before he followed, Brenik scanned the ground below and his eyes widened with fright. Bones had been thrown and scattered across the lush greensward that was now splattered in blood. The jovkins must have torn the bodies apart, ate what they wanted, and disposed of the bones like they were nothing.

Brenik didn't want to worry Bray, so he leaped off the gnarled branch and trailed near her to search for the Stone of Desire. He kept his thoughts away from Junah and what lay ahead, because it would have to be better than the death that awaited them if they remained in Laith.

Together they flew and they flew, through the blend of trees that were all a blur except the leaves' embodiment of color that warped Brenik's vision. Time had no meaning until the sound of water flowing awoke him from his trance. Slowly, Brenik let his wings lessen their movement right as Brayora did the same.

A large white boulder slid into view. "Brayora, look! I think that is it," he called.

His sister's head twisted back to him, then whipped around to where he was frantically pointing. "You are right, little brother. That has to be it."

Higher and higher Brenik flew, until he could tell the structure on top of the stone was the shape of a rose. The rock was bright white and dark shadows danced around it under the twin suns' specks of light. Already, they were in the process of setting to make room for the twin moons to rise.

Closer. He needed to draw closer. Swishing his wings back and forth, slower and slower, he let his body descend toward the top of the rock's creases before landing in between two folds. Shortly after, Brayora dwindled down beside him.

Kneeling on the rough stone, Brenik lifted his hand to press it to the grain at the same time as Bray whispered, "Put your hand against it like Junah said."

"I know," he shot back, scowling. She did not need to remind him how to do everything. Her expression told him she was sorry, yet she still monitored his movements closely.

Brenik smacked his hand against the boulder while his sister gently pressed down on it. Shifting his focus from the rock to Bray's face, Brenik found no answer of what was to come. Her gaze penetrated the rock as if she was trying to command it to move—but everything was *not* commanded by her like she thought it was.

At that precise moment, a hard quake knocked Brenik backward. He struck the right side of his wing against the rough edge of the rock fold. *Maybe she does command everything.* He rubbed the tip of his wing where it throbbed, then hopped off the Stone. Bray repeated his motions and lingered close beside him.

His hands rested by his sides, fingers fluttering with nervousness, when another vibration from the Stone shook the ground. Dirt surrounding the white rose rock slithered away in broken fragments.

Bray appeared to be the epitome of calm, while Brenik wanted to fly back to Junah to let her know what had occurred. His heart pounded and ached at having to leave Junah. But no matter what, he could not go back. The jovkins could already be making their way to where Junah was.

The large rock ascended from the ground as a consistent convulsion shook the surrounding trees. Birds rapidly chirped above them, then stormed away, causing a few crunchy brown leaves to rain down upon Brenik.

Bray and Brenik floated to the ground. The jolting noises stopped after the rock had grown into something new, almost oval-like. It stayed perfectly still, unmoving. Then it happened. It awakened, unfolding from different areas: long, thin legs emerged from the bottom—alabaster stone arms appeared from the sides. A head poked forward like a turtle coming out of its shell, and the rose structure seemed to glide downward to cover its back.

At the sight of the Stone's head, Brenik took two steps back. Shaking, Brenik gritted his teeth and bit the side of his tongue to make it bleed, so he could focus on something else. The two eyelids of the Stone leisurely opened to reveal eyes the color of raven wings. No nose. No mouth. But somehow it spoke in a voice that was low and deep.

"What do you desire?" The voice didn't come from outside, it came directly inside Brenik's head.

Bray's lips parted, seeming startled, too. Neither one of them said anything to each other, both only focused on the creature in front of them.

"What do you desire?" the voice boomed inside Brenik's skull once again. Burning flames seemed to lick inside his head. He lifted his hands and placed them against his temples to try and make the stinging sensation stop.

Bray, ever the brave one, spoke up for the both of them. "A jovkin named Junah sent us here and said you may be able to send us away—somewhere safe."

Tilting its head to the sky, then gingerly angling it down, the Stone crawled toward them. "So, you want me to save you. Why should I do this?"

"Please, I want you to help my brother. Harbor us, but most of all protect him." Bray fell to her knees in pleading.

"And you?" The Stone's head shifted lower until it was just a hair's breadth from Brenik's face.

"Yes, please save me. I—I won't be able to survive if you leave me here."

"What about your sister?"

"Yes," he rushed the words out. "Her, too." He did not want to be separated from his sister on the journey, and he would not leave without her.

Suddenly, the Stone shuffled backward. Brenik thought the Stone would leave them both there, but then it spoke, "I will grant access, but only because of her—how badly she wants to save you. She is pure and will be granted a gift to survive where I will be sending the both of you. If you agree, you may pass."

Brenik did not understand why Bray was to be granted a gift and not him. His shoulders slumped, and his heart sank because this was how it always was and always would be. Again, he was only second best. But for their escape, he would agree to anything. "We agree," he murmured.

The Stone of Desire nodded and slid a hand across the dirt, flipping its palm upward for them. Brenik stepped onto the stone with his bare feet pressed against the roughness, while Bray flew down toward the middle, grabbing his hand.

Brenik's body quivered as the arm coasted backward, afraid they were going to be eaten. But since the creature had no mouth, he was not sure how that would be possible. They were pulled under and farther back into the depths of shadows, until there was a flash of white light, followed by another bout of darkness.

Two

Bray
Present Day, 1995

Bray tossed the note against the tree wall and let out a frustrated sigh. He left again. The drawing from the letter played over in her head: a basic sketch of their tree, and Brenik flying away from it. That meant he would be gone for a while.

Should I be so desperate for him to stay? Just because I want him to? she thought. Brenik was her brother, and he should be able to go off whenever he wanted. But she was so alone here. *Ruth.* Bray couldn't think about her either. Ruth was gone—had been gone for a year.

This world was supposed to be so much better than Laith and for a time, it was, until it wasn't. Brenik had been distant since Ruth died, and now Bray was completely alone. She lay back down on her silky yellow hammock and tilted her head up toward the roof of the tree, staring at the words she and Brenik had carved in the ceiling over the years. Their first word was *Junah*, so they would always remember her, and the next was *Laith*, to remind them where they had come from. The last word they carved was *Ruth* because she had given them everything. Brenik would always stand close by as Bray carved each word with care.

No new words since then.

A shuffling sound ripped Bray from her torturous thoughts. It sounded like Ruth was in her garden, but she reminded herself that Ruth would *never* plant any bushes or flowers again.

More stirring—the sound of digging—spread through the tree. Bray leaped from the hammock and crept to the edge of the hole to peer out, just as she heard a loud grunt. A shovel struck the ground, and two filthy hands held the tool in his sweaty grip. No shirt, a headful of brown hair that fell past his earlobes, and no face. Well, he did have a face, but Bray couldn't see it yet.

Quietly, Bray pulled her small body from the edge and tightened her dark wings against her back, prepared to flee.

Though she was practically on her stomach, Bray lifted her head back up to peep out of the hole to get a better look. Natural brown skin reflected the sun's rays, and the guy was lean with well-defined muscle—but not to the point where it was ridiculous.

Turning away from Mystery Face, Bray discovered he had a whole garden waiting to be planted: white roses, yellow daisies, and green bushes. She had no idea what the last ones really were, so she would just call them green bushes. Ruth had a beautiful garden once, until everything died, along with her.

"Hey, I'm heading to school now. I'll see you after," a voice called from farther away. Bray's gaze automatically turned to the back of the house where a small boy—who must have been about seven—stood. Bray wasn't very good at guessing ages, so maybe he was six. She wasn't sure. His haircut looked like a bowl sitting on the top of his head with the hair parted and split smoothly down the center. It wasn't as bad as some of the hairstyles she had seen when she used to watch TV with Ruth and Brenik, though. The boy's baggy striped shirt fell to his knees, almost the same length as his shorts, hiding the remainder of his thin upper arms and legs.

"Okay, Lu. Do you want me to drive you today?" Mystery Face twisted his neck to look over his shoulder at the little kid. Not a mystery anymore. His face was nice, matching the kid's younger one. *Might be about twenty-five, possibly had the kid a little young*, she decided.

"No, I like the walk." The kid smiled wildly and shifted the backpack on his shoulder.

Nice Face set down the shovel and walked closer to the kid. "You sure, Luca? I'm about to head off to work, and it's on the way."

"I got this. I gotta learn to take care of myself."

Nice Face's expression turned into not such a nice face. "Someone bothering you at school?"

"No, just gotta impress." The boy's—who Nice Face had called Luca—wild smile became a bit tamer and practically said there was no bullying to worry about.

"O—kay," Nice Face said almost skeptically, studying the kid for a few extra seconds. His tight shoulders seemed to relax a fraction. "Well, I'll be home around four, so see you then. Love you."

"Love you, too." Luca pivoted on his heels and gave Nice Face a tilt of the head goodbye.

Nice Face picked the shovel back up off the ground and resumed his digging. Bray wondered where the mom was— probably already at work. Ruth's house had been sitting there for a long time with a for sale sign in the front yard until about a month ago. Bray guessed the new family was finally there and must have moved in the day before.

Growing bored of watching the guy dig holes, Bray crawled away from the open space and stood. She crashed down on the hammock, letting it sway her back and forth. *What is on the list of things for me to do today?* she wondered. *Oh, that's right, my usual—sleep*. If Brenik was there, they would probably just sit in silence—at least that was better than being completely alone.

Bray wasn't sure how long she had drifted off for, but a puddle of wetness rested against her cheek when she woke up. *Okay, so it's only drool from myself.* Lifting a hand up toward her cheek, she swiped the saliva away and rubbed it on to the hammock. *Classy,* she thought, but there was already some gathered there anyway.

Remembering the events from earlier, Bray headed straight to the hole and peeked out. She shifted her head from left to right. *Nothing.* Bray looked up and down, noticing a few bushes had already been planted in the dirt.

Then she saw it: a circular stone bowl filled with water sitting on top of a long thick stem, attached to a circular bottom. *A birdbath!* With a huge grin, Bray stepped on the ledge of the hole and leaped off, flapping her wings hurriedly to the nearest pink and yellow peach. Opening her jaw wide, she bit into the thin skin. A juicy one. The fruit filled her mouth with delicious pleasure, and she took one more long bite before diving down to the birdbath.

The top of her newfound treasure was a perfect circle with tiny mounds around it resembling hills. Bray landed on the ceramic and bent down to take a seat, before placing her bare feet into the warm water that had been thoroughly heated from the gleaming sun.

Peering down at the clear water, Bray saw no sign of intrusion from other creatures yet. She rotated her head in every direction, as if she would be caught just by thinking about slipping into the water—still no sign of life.

Flicking her braid over her shoulder, Bray pursed her lips together to hide the smile shining against her face and jumped into the water. The splash echoed. Her bare feet scraped the rough bottom, while her dress inflated and then clung to her body as she shot to the surface. She let out a small giggle to herself. It was sad that the only highlight of the past year was hopping into a shallow pool of water with no one around except for her.

She leaned back into the liquid, floating and moving her arms slowly up and down, while swimming in figure-eight circles.

Bray closed her eyes and let the water cover her ears, so that nothing in the world existed, except for the muffled vibrations from the liquid.

A loud boom startled Bray out of her daydreams and her eyes flew open to meet two dark irises, warm brown skin, and that black bowl hair.

Tiny human.

Luca.

Freeze, Bray thought to herself, not even blinking her eyes. She held them wide open, thinking he wouldn't notice her, or maybe he would just assume she was a bird. Even though he was staring at her and had spoken something she didn't hear clearly.

Nope. That isn't going to work. He hovered closer, his eyes scrunched halfway closed to examine her more thoroughly. Unable to hold her lids open any longer, Bray blinked several times.

"What are you?" he asked, genuine amazement creeping into his words, his lips slightly parted.

"A bat!" Bray yelled, and she jumped up from the warmth of the water, darting straight for the tree hole.

Chest heaving, Bray landed inside and collided with the floor. She rolled to her back, running both hands down her face. "Why did I come out without paying attention? I know not to!" Ruth had always told her this.

A quake trembled through the tree, causing shivers to run

up and down her spine. *What is the little beast doing? Oh no, what if he's trying to chop down the tree? My home—the peaches!* Bray didn't know why she was thinking about stupid peaches when there was another fruit tree directly next door.

Despite the thunderous rumbling, Bray grabbed the needle from underneath her hammock and dodged toward the window. If the little beast thought he could take her down, then he had another thing coming. She would prick his eye—actually, she would poke both of his eyes to protect her and Brenik's home.

When Bray reached the edge of the window, the sound stopped. She peeped her head out of the hole, right as a face met hers, his black hair falling forward over a hazel eye—an eye she was going to poke. Startled, she jumped back instead of toward him.

A broad smile crossed the little beast's face. "Hello."

Freezing once again, until she remembered that the staying-still-as-a-statue strategy didn't work in the birdbath, she meekly said, "Hi."

Bray brought the needle up toward his smiling face, just in case.

"Are you planning on sewing something?" He tilted his head at the needle.

"Yeah, your eyeball." She gave him a hard glare.

"What?" he asked while laughing hysterically.

He was laughing? Not scared? Bray brought the needle closer. "You need to leave and never come back. This is *my* home."

"No. Technically, it's my brother's home," he said, still smiling.

"What brother? You mean your dad who was planting out there this morning?"

Luca shook his head, and she didn't miss the wince before he spoke. "No, that's my brother, Wes. I don't have a mom or dad."

Stomach sinking, Bray lowered the needle. "Oh. Me neither. I only have a brother, but he will be gone for a while." She paused and glanced at the note Brenik had left behind, her chest tightening. Then she shrugged it off and shifted her gaze back to the boy. "By the way, my name is Brayora, but you can call me Bray." For some reason, she wasn't worried anymore about the human.

"I'm Luca Duran." He plopped his thin fingers on the edge of the hole.

"Yeah, I heard your name this morning, little beast. I mean, Luca." She thought little beast suited him better than Luca.

"Little beast?" He grinned.

"Sorry, I thought you were trying to tear down the tree." Softly, she lifted his fingers from the ledge of the hole.

"Um, I don't think I could do that without an ax. I'm not *that* strong." He seemed strong enough to her, even though he was much smaller than his brother.

"How old are you anyway? Six?"

Pulling his head back from the tree, Luca straightened his neck and narrowed his eyes. "What? I just turned ten and am in the fifth grade," he said proudly.

"Six… Ten… Same difference." Human children his age all appeared the same to her.

Luca cocked his head, as if trying to look older than he was. "No, six is a baby. I'm no baby."

"You can keep on thinking that." Bray laughed and set the needle back on the floor.

"How old are you?"

Bray tugged her shoulders back. "I'm twenty."

"So you're old then, like my brother. He's twenty-three."

Scowling, Bray placed her hands on her hips and took a step toward him. "What? I'm not old!"

"My mom was nineteen when she had Wes, so it would definitely make you old."

Bray wasn't sure how old her mother was when she had her

and Brenik.

"I'm going to ignore that statement," she huffed.

"Well, see ya." Luca started heading down the tree, limb by limb.

"Wait! That's it?" Bray dove out, flapping her wings, and halting in front of Luca's face as his feet struck the ground.

"I need to eat a snack. I'm starving and just got home from school." He brushed a few beads of perspiration away from his forehead.

Her stomach growled at the word *snack*, and it was loud enough for Luca to hear.

He hiked his thumb back at the door. "Do you want to come in?"

"No. I don't want to be seen," she said half-heartedly. It was enough for one person to see her today, but it also felt good to have someone to talk to. Her gaze kept training on the door, and Luca didn't miss it.

"Wes isn't home yet—and don't worry, I won't tell him." He held his hand up in front of her face and crossed his index and middle finger.

One tiny human who seemed trustworthy enough shouldn't be a problem. Bray plopped down on Luca's shoulder like they had known each other for an eternity, and he walked inside the house—Ruth's house.

Except it looked nothing like her home anymore and hadn't in a very long time. After it was cleared out, Bray never went back inside. Now, there were cardboard boxes sprawled across the large living room. Against the wall was a floral couch, and diagonal from it rested two blue sitting chairs. A large box TV was propped in the center of the room, pushed up to the opposite wall. Bray ached to turn it on because it had been so long since she had used one.

Luca took out two blueberry muffins from the tiny pantry in the kitchen, padded into the living room, and set the wrappers on a rectangular wooden coffee table across from the sofa.

Flipping on the television, Luca shuffled to the VHS tapes and popped one in that was already halfway through the movie. He swiveled back around and opened the muffin wrapper for Bray. She landed on the coffee table and focused on eating the blueberry part first.

"So you're a fairy, like from *Peter Pan*?" Luca asked, while he stuffed most of the muffin into his mouth, letting small crumbs fall into his lap.

"No, I'm a bat." Bray angled her head in the direction of the TV and pointed furiously at the furry creature with big ears on the screen. "Hey, we have those in Laith."

"A Mogwai?" Luca's eyes bulged with excitement.

"What? No, a drogwai." She had no idea what a Mogwai was, but that creature on the screen looked incredibly similar to a drogwai.

"Okay, well, Gizmo is a Mogwai," Luca corrected.

"That is incorrect."

"I'll take your word for it, since you say you're a *bat* and all," he said with sarcasm lacing each word, and a big smile spreading, showing a row of crooked bottom teeth.

Bray's lips tugged to the side, and she opened her mouth to speak when a car door slammed shut outside. Her chest tightened, making it difficult to breathe. She had to get out of there.

"Crap, Wes is home. Hurry!" Luca sprinted for the back door, tearing it open, and gesturing for Bray to escape. She zoomed out without a proper goodbye and pumped her wings as hard as she could toward the tree hole, until her body slammed against the floor.

Hurriedly, while still out of breath, Bray gazed out the hole and saw Luca giving her a thumbs up from the glass window before heading back to his brother.

Three

Brenik
Ten Years Ago

A bright white light seeped through the darkness, and a sudden shake erupted beneath Brenik's feet. He turned toward Bray, but he could not see her face, only an outline. Still, he heard her whisper softly, "It will be okay, little brother."

He nodded in the dissipating darkness as the Stone of Desire's arm pushed them farther and farther out toward the light. Brenik's heart had not ceased pounding, and it needed more oxygen than his own lungs did.

Skyscraping trees appeared in his vision: green and brown. They were tall and full of needle-like leaves he had never seen before.

"Pine trees," Brayora whispered as her blue eyes sparkled under the light. "Junah told me about how we have them on the other side of Laith." Yet he and his sister were no longer in Laith.

Junah had never discussed those things with him, but he had never asked her about leaves either. "Where are we?" he demanded, clasping his hands together while digging his index finger into the skin of the opposite hand.

"You are on Earth," the loud voice of the Stone boomed in Brenik's head. He whirled around to see its face had already closed in.

The Stone tilted its alabaster hand, and Brenik and Bray slid down until their backsides hit the dew-covered grass. Leaping up from the moisture, Brenik brushed the dirt from his wings.

"What do we do now?" Bray inquired, calmly flicking a blade of grass from her brown dress.

"You try and live. The female will have the gift of survival." Without another word, the Stone of Desire withdrew and curled itself back into the rose-shaped boulder, tucking its head in first, followed by arms and legs. A low grumbling penetrated the air as the Stone slowly sank into the dirt. The ground shook beneath their feet for several of Brenik's heartbeats, until the Stone looked the same as when they first discovered it in Laith.

Running a hand through his shoulder-length black hair, Brenik turned to Bray and asked, "What do we do now? The Stone said you have the gift of survival, so what is it?" He could not understand why the Stone did not let them know what it was. A large part of him desperately wanted to go back home.

Bray's nose crinkled as she mulled it over. "I—I don't know. I don't feel any differently." She took off on a sprint toward the rose stone and slammed her palm against it. Nothing happened. "Come back! I have more questions."

The realization that maybe they should have stayed in Laith washed over Brenik. Shaking his head, he ran up beside Bray to set his hand beside hers on top of the cool stone. *Nothing. Nothing. Nothing.*

Bray took a couple of steps back and turned around to take in the scene before them. "One sun. Look, Brenik, there is only one sun in the sky here." She tugged on the edge of his brown tunic and pointed a finger at the light blue sky.

Astonishment buried itself inside his chest as he gazed up

at it. "The sky is blue! Not a pale pink like Laith's sky, but *blue*." It was beautiful. Enormous, white puffy clouds were pressed into the sky that contrasted with Laith's, which were the darkest of grays.

Flapping his inky wings, with the wind dance against his face, Brenik soared up to the top of a tree to look out as far as he could. Sharp points pricked his skin from the tips of the needle leaves, and he backed away in annoyance, a slight stinging sensation lingering on his arm.

Bray appeared next to him, scanning the foliage, almost meticulously. "We have to be careful—we don't know what species this place has. What if they are worse than Junah's kind?"

He could practically feel the blood boiling in his body, unable to hold the displeasure back. "Quit acting like you are in charge all the time, Brayora. I know what I am doing. I am not a youngling anymore, so stop treating me as such."

Bray's eyes glistened, and Brenik swallowed thickly at the sight. He knew instantly that he shouldn't have yelled at her. But there was also a little bliss at seeing the hurt there—maybe she would understand now how he felt.

"I am sorry, I did not mean to yell at you like that. It is because I already miss Junah, and I am not sure what to do." This was an unfamiliar place, and he had to learn new things— the idea frightened him.

In understanding, she smiled as she nodded, and they decided to fly through the trees until they found something to eat. There were birds and insects, but he could not find one fruit tree anywhere in sight. A gurgling sound rumbled from Brenik's stomach, and they flew until the edge of the forest neared, where there were no more trees to pass through.

Descending to the ground, Brenik's feet hit a hardened gray surface. "What is this?" he asked Bray as her bare feet thumped down beside his.

Leaning forward to inspect the gray color, Bray crawled on

the surface, as if she was trying to get a real feel for it. "I don't know, but what are these white lines in the middle?" She bent her head down, letting her nose touch one of the white shapes, and breathed deeply.

Brayora wasn't paying attention as a loud roar filled the air—a demonic black beast barreled toward her. Brenik lunged forward as fast as he could and yanked Bray back before the monstrosity collided with her. They tumbled backward into the grass, and he released her to stand up. Anger pulsed in his veins. If she had gotten herself killed, he would have been all alone because of her stupidity.

"What were you doing crawling on the ground like that? Not paying attention!" he spat.

Bray tossed her long, black braid over her shoulder, and it fell back to her waist. "Calm down, little brother, I am okay." Yet he could tell by her heavy breaths his sister wasn't.

"You are only okay because of me! You could have died!" he yelled. "And what *was* that?" He had never seen something that stormed with such intense fury. The jovkins were fast, but not quite like that.

"I don't know, but it did not see us." Bray's breaths were slightly ragged, and Brenik knew she was as frightened as he was.

"Where have you brought us to? I want to go back home!" Brenik balled his hands into tight fists at his sides, staring hard at Bray, but she was peering at something else.

"Look over there, Brenik. Peaches!" His gaze turned to where she was pointing, and he spotted a tree full of the delicious fruit.

Bray kept her focus on the tree as she walked back to the gray surface. Her movements came to an abrupt halt, and she let out a loud wail.

Brenik's body jolted, and he rushed up beside her, heart beating frantically against his lungs. "What is wrong?"

The color red. Her foot was dripping with blood. Bray lifted it off the ground, her blue eyes filling with tears as she and Brenik saw the small, clear objects embedded in the soft flesh. Horror struck him, not knowing what was attacking Bray's foot or what it could do to her.

"Let's head to a tree, and I'll take a look at it there. I am fine." Bray did not look fine, but she took off before he could get a word out.

As Brenik approached the tree, he noticed a row on the ground of what looked to be some form of enormous shelters, and not like the ones that existed back in Laith.

Brenik's focus fell to Bray when he landed beside her, who already had her back firmly pressed against the trunk of the tree.

Tears slid down the sides of her face as she studied her foot. One of the tiny objects was poking out, so Brenik swiftly removed it. Bray let out a tiny gasp and pursed her lips tightly shut. Blood oozed out, and Brenik thought he may have made a mistake.

Out of nowhere, a shadow stretched over them. Brenik was scared to look up, but he did it anyway. The shadow formed into a body that was not a bat like them, and nothing like Junah's horned kind, yet it was distinctly female. The top of her ears had no pointed tips like theirs, but curved ones instead.

"Have I just entered the land of Thumbelina? I must be dreaming." The female creature reached out to pinch her wrinkled wrist—the skin hung loosely, covered in spots of various shades of brown. Gray hair sat upon her head in short, tight curls, and she wore a white dress covered in daffodils.

Brenik was about to fly off, when Bray pulled him back. His sister straightened her spine, her voice calm and unafraid as she spoke. "I am Brayora and this is my brother Brenik. We came here from Laith." Brenik could not bring himself to say a single word.

The female shook her head several times, seeming to come

out of her trance. Her wrinkled hand gripped the front of her flowered dress, and she took several steps back. "This ain't real. I'm just seein' things. This happens when you get old, and by the light of day, I am old. Seventy-two to be exact. This is it. I'm gettin' Alzheimer's, ain't I? Senile like Jimmy was before he passed."

Brenik and Bray sat together, bodies pressed as far back against the tree as they could go. Something sharp jabbed Brenik's shoulder, but he ignored it. All he could do was listen to the withered creature mumble to herself.

Slowly rising off the ground, Bray flapped her wings to approach the creature. "Hello, I am Brayora." His sister had already told the female that, but he assumed she needed to repeat herself for some strange reason.

The female hadn't responded yet, only stared at Brayora.

"What are you?" Bray asked.

"I—I am a woman, a human which you seem not to be. Yer a fairy."

Brenik cringed. That was *not* what they were, and it was humiliating that she would think them to be such pitiful creatures. Junah had spun tales about fairies to them back in Laith.

"Close, but not quite. We are bats," Bray said proudly.

Mouth agape, the human nodded. "Okay, then. Maybe a bat without hair." Her eyes shifted to Bray's injured foot. In a flash, the human's face changed from nervousness to concern. "What happened?" Gasping, the woman reached out and snatched Bray's foot. Apprehension pulsed at Brenik's insides, but he did not move. Instead, he was thinking about a plan of attack.

"I don't know—I stepped on something on the gray surface." Bray pointed in the direction of where the injury occurred.

"You were in the street?" the woman shrieked.

"Maybe?" Bray did not seem to know, and Brenik was not

sure either.

Inching closer, the woman pulled some form of instrument out of her shirt pocket and placed it over her eyes—the object seemed to help her see better. "It looks to be glass. We better get this out so you don't catch anything. Not sure if you can get somethin' like tetanus from glass like you could from a rusty nail. Can you wait right here? I'll go inside and get some supplies, dearie."

Trustworthy Brayora nodded without any worry lines on her face. The woman headed back inside, and Bray wiggled closer to Brenik. "She is going to help me, little brother."

"How do you even know that? How do you know she is not just going to eat us?" He did not think the human would really eat them, since she had already held Bray and could have taken a bite of her appendage then.

Despite her being the injured one, Bray stuck out a hand and placed it on Brenik's shoulder, giving him a soft pat. "I have a good feeling about her."

"Is this the gift of survival the Stone told us about?" Maybe Bray could see who was good and who was not.

"Possibly." She shrugged.

A squeak radiated outside when the old woman returned from her shelter with a handful of objects. Quickly, the human knelt on the ground, and Brenik clenched the grass in between his fingers to calm himself down. Brayora was already crawling across the grass to inspect the objects as the woman lined them in a neat row.

Pointing at each object, the woman told them what they were. "I've got a tweezer, alcohol, cotton balls, antibiotic cream, and some bandages. Ain't nothin' special, but it's the best I can do."

Brayora crawled nearer.

"You've gotta come closer than that, dearie, since yer foot is so small. Even with these glasses it's hard to see at my old age. By the way, my name's Ruth. I must have forgotten to tell you two that in the process of being scared to death. In fact, I think I might still be dreaming.”

Glasses. That was what the instrument covering her eyes was called. Brenik found them interesting.

Bray rolled onto her back and lifted her foot into the air as Ruth grabbed the tweezers. Holding Bray’s foot steady, she rubbed against her heel with the tweezers, and Bray let out a high-pitched giggle.

“Aren’t you the cutest thing I ever did see.” Ruth laughed in return.

Frustration sewed its way through Brenik’s bloodstream. Bray was already being favored once again. But then Ruth’s head tilted down, her big eyes meeting his, and she gave him a warm smile. “And you, aren’t you the most beautiful tiny prince I ever did see.”

“I am Brenik,” he said while tipping his chin up with pride at being called a prince, which would be considered on a higher level than *thing*.

With the tweezer still in her hand, Ruth pointed between Brenik and Bray’s foot. “Are you gonna sit over there all day, Prince Brenik, or are you gonna help me with this little lassie’s foot?”

“She is my sister,” he grunted as he flew and landed on Ruth’s wrinkled wrist.

“Well, tiny prince, I am gonna have you help me since I can’t see all that well. Point to all the pieces, then I’ll dig ‘em out.”

Brenik didn’t have to be asked twice. He felt needed as he helped Ruth find each small fragment of glass. There were four in all, and one minuscule piece she had to scrape at several times to retrieve.

When Ruth was finished, she cleansed the area with the alcohol and a cotton ball, followed by adding the cream and strapping on the bandage.

After Brenik told Ruth they knew nothing of this realm, she

took them inside her home to give a lesson about Earth. Ruth said she was going to teach them everything she knew—from reading to the world in general. But they couldn't ever show themselves out in the open, and they were lucky to have stumbled upon her. She switched on a box she called the television, and that was their first lesson.

"Welcome to Texas." Ruth grinned. "People love TV."

Four

Bray
Present Day, 1995

After scurrying out of Luca's house, Bray sat inside the tree for a while, not knowing what to do. She wished Brenik were there—he would have probably had them abandon their home and find somewhere else to live, since Bray had been seen.

But Brenik wasn't there, and Bray was a much more curious person than he was. The night had already spread its dark blanket on the world when she peered out from the hole. Fluttering out of her home, Bray dove to a peach to get a few bites to fill her stomach. The fruit wasn't as juicy as the one from earlier, yet she didn't mind because the sweet taste still fulfilled her.

At the back of the house, a light shined from one of the bedroom windows. Bray angled her head to try and see inside. The master bedroom's lone window attached to the side of the house, so she assumed this one must belong to Luca. Ruth always said curiosity killed the cat, but Bray wasn't a cat, so she flew toward the lighted window.

A thin gap rested between the white laced curtains and she could see Luca's black head leaning over a book, reading. No sign of his brother Wes.

Bray lightly tapped the window—he didn't hear it. So she poked at the window again. Nothing. Harder this time, she struck the glass twice and that got Luca's attention. He craned his fragile neck toward the window, his expression blank.

Then she tapped it three times, and he slowly rose from the bed and walked to the window, tearing the curtains away from the glass. Giving a quick wave, Bray smiled at him, and Luca shook his head as he opened the window.

"What are you doing?" Luca whispered and closed the window as she flew in toward a tall wooden shelf, positioned against the wall across from the bed. Books of all shapes and sizes were neatly tucked in organized lines.

"I was hoping you had a TV in here," she said while poring over all the book titles, her eyes roaming over each and every spine.

Ruth taught Bray and Brenik how to read, not that Brenik had enjoyed it much since he had struggled with the activity, but Bray loved it—still did.

Whirling around to find Luca watching her from the humongous bed, she rushed over to the book beside him. "What are you reading?"

"*Peter Pan.*" He lifted the book to show her the cover with a boy in green tights, flying through the air with specks of gold dust trailing behind him. She loved *Peter Pan.*

"Aren't you a little old for *Peter Pan*?" she teased.

"*What*? Wes loves this book, and he's the one who's old."

"Oh, right. I forgot I'm ancient." She smiled and wondered why it was only Luca and Wes living together in Ruth's house. "What happened to your parents?" She didn't know if he would feel uncomfortable about the question, but she had no filter when it came to asking things.

Luca didn't even pause to think about it or seem bothered about her asking. "When I was four, my parents were visiting Mexico where my dad was from—they died in a car wreck.

My grandpa who lived here took care of us after that—he died three years ago, so now it's just me and Wes."

Her stomach sank. "I'm so sorry."

"I don't remember my parents much, and I do miss my grandpa. But, Wes is the one who's been around the longest—he's been like a dad to me."

Bray wasn't sure what else to say because at least he had a brother who was around—hers was always gone these days doing who knew what.

Her gaze fell to the book now laying in Luca's lap. "Would you want to read some of *Peter Pan* to me?"

With a huge smile, Luca snatched the book up and opened it to the beginning. "It's pretty much like I'm Peter Pan and you're Tinker Bell, since Tinker was, you know … *old*," he taunted.

Stifling a laugh, Bray told him to open the book and just read. He propped his pillow up against the headboard of the bed and scooched back to a more comfortable reading position. Bray flew to his upper body, curling up on his shoulder while listening to his small voice read each enchanting line of the story. Bray and Brenik had always done the same thing with Ruth, except Bray would sit on one side of her shoulder and Brenik on the other as their caretaker read to them.

Yawning, Bray glanced up toward Luca's face—he had fallen asleep, the book sprawled open on his lap. A small pattern of freckles spread across his nose and upper cheeks, and he appeared to be a lot younger than his ten years. She still wanted to say he looked six.

Bray was too tired to figure out a way to escape his room, and she didn't want to wake his tired frame, so she folded herself up into a tight ball against his shoulder. Closing her eyes, Bray wished she had a little brother like him, along with Brenik.

"What the *hell* is that?" a loud voice yelled, disturbing Bray from her slumber. "Luca, stay perfectly still. I think there's a bat on your shoulder."

Keeping her face hidden, Bray stayed in statue mode as Luca stirred from his sleep. "What, Wes?" he asked groggily.

"Don't. Move. *Rabies.*" Each word was slow and filled with paranoia.

Okay, before this becomes any crazier, Bray thought as she unfolded her stiff wings and adjusted herself into a sitting position on Luca's shoulder. "I. Do. Not. Have. Rabies."

"What the *fuck*?" Wes slammed his back against the wall, causing the bookshelf to wobble. Shaking away his surprised expression, he looked at Luca, who was just sitting there on the bed rotating his head side to side between Wes and Bray.

"Luca, I'm going to knock the thing off your shoulder and then you hurry over here." Wes took a few small steps toward them.

"Wes, she's not a bat." Luca held up both his hands. "I mean, she is, but she isn't a bat like what we have here. Do you understand?"

"No! I don't understand! It just *talked*. It isn't a bat!"

Bray had heard enough of the conversation and flew off Luca's shoulder toward Wes, staring into his dark brown eyes. She crossed her arms. "Yes, I *am* a bat."

Wes pointed at Bray with his index finger. "You are *not* a bat. You have a face." Bringing up his hand, he made a circular motion in front of his own face, attempting to emphasize his point.

It didn't work.

Narrowing her eyes, Bray drew nearer to the ridiculous human. "I. Am. A. Bat."

A deep crease settled between his dark brows. "This is

fucked up." Whipping his eyes over to Luca, he said, "I'm sorry, Luca. I shouldn't be using this language around you, but what is seriously going on? Am I *hallucinating*?"

Wes padded to the mattress and sat beside Luca.

"Wes, I met her this morning in the garden, swimming around in the new birdbath."

"What?" Confusion crossed Wes's face, and he slid a hand down the side of his head, turning his attention in Bray's direction. "So, you're a bird, then? Not a bat."

Placing her hands on her hips, annoyed, Bray asked, "Is that sarcasm?"

"No, it's not sarcasm, but if you say you're a *bat* and then go parading around in a birdbath, what the hell am I supposed to think? Like I said, you have a face—a body—and *wings*."

If Bray's hand was large enough at that moment, she would have smacked the human across his face—hard.

"Then to top it off," he added, "you were sitting on Luca's shoulder, practically sucking his blood." He placed his hands gently on Luca's cheeks and tilted the boy's head to the side, checking to make sure there were no bitemarks.

Bray rolled her eyes and inched closer to the bed. "I don't have fangs—not long ones anyway." She opened her mouth and tapped at a sharp canine tooth. Wes's scowl only deepened.

Luca blinked and studied Wes. "Why are you even in here?"

"Because you left the light on, Lu." Wes shook his head as if he just answered the dumbest question in all of Laith—*no*—Earth. "You aren't the least bit freaked out about whatever it is that's going on here?"

"No, Bray's nice."

Wes whipped his head over his shoulder to face her. "*Bray*?"

"I said *he* could call me Bray. You will have to call me Brayora." She was finding it increasingly difficult to stay calm, her fingers and toes twitching.

"I won't be calling you anything except for—you need to go away to wherever you came from," Wes said hastily.

Bray cocked her head in the direction of the window and arched a brow. "Well, open the window then—and I'll fly back to my tree."

"What tree?" Wes didn't even follow the direction in which she was looking. *How could one human have such an appalling lack of manners?*

"The only tree in the backyard." She motioned at the one window in the room *again,* in case he truly didn't understand. He still didn't look. "What other tree do you think I'm talking about?"

"There are trees right next door on either side of the house."

"Whatever." Wes knew which tree she had been talking about. He was trying to make things difficult.

"She can't go back out there—she'll get cold," Luca said while pretending to shiver. Bray found it hard to hold back a smile.

Wes rolled his eyes and rubbed at his temples. "It's seventy degrees outside, Luca."

"Exactly." Luca gave Wes a pointed look.

"I'm fine. I've been sleeping out there for a whole year." Bray and Brenik would sleep inside the house most of the time with Ruth, but they had also slept out in the tree sometimes because they'd loved listening to all the night sounds that reminded them of Laith.

"Where did you sleep before?" Wes asked, bewildered.

"In here. The tree was just a place where we could relax. We would sleep and stay inside this house most of the time."

"We?" Wes's puzzled expression became even more confused.

"My brother and I." At that moment, Bray wished Brenik was there to help her explain things.

"There are more of you?" Wes hurried to the window,

squinted his eyes and looked in the direction of the peach tree that was now camouflaged by the darkness.

"Only the two of us," Bray assured him. "The rest are in Laith—or were." Bray had no idea if any bats were left—she had never seen any others besides Brenik and her mother.

Bray gazed at the ceiling and told them the story of how she and Brenik escaped their world and came to Earth. How a wonderful woman named Ruth took them in and taught her and Brenik so much—until she passed away.

"See, Wes," Luca started, "this house really must belong to her, then. We can't let her go back to sleeping outside."

"Um—yes, we can," Wes answered without pause.

"No, we can't!" Luca argued.

"I'm fine, really," Bray said. She had been fine for a while, if not a little lonely.

Wes took a few steps toward her. "Look, Bray…"

"Brayora," she muttered.

"Right. Since Luca is set on you staying here for the night, and I'm still not sure if this is even real—you can, but you can't sleep in here with him."

"Why? Because she's twenty?" Luca asked.

"You're twenty?" Wes just could not get rid of that confused expression.

"Yes," she answered.

"Okay, then two reasons: you're twenty and you have wings." Bray and Luca didn't say anything. "For tonight, you're going to have to sleep in my room because I still don't trust you. Nothing against you *per se*—I wouldn't trust a dog the first night either."

Bray wanted to say that she wasn't anything like a dog, but kept her mouth shut. She shrugged and told Luca good night, then darted off to the master bedroom. As she entered Ruth's old space, she didn't bother to glance around at the new décor before crashing at the edge of the large bed.

She could have gone outside for the night, but the feeling

of being inside the house once again brought back the good nostalgic moments of the past. Bray hadn't thought she needed to feel it again, but she did.

Wes and Luca's hushed voices echoed through the wall, but she couldn't understand what was being said. Moments later, Wes entered the room wearing a white shirt and a pair of plaid boxers that she hadn't paid attention to earlier. Bray turned her head away from him, still angry that he inferred she had rabies.

Bray knew exactly what rabies were—Ruth watched the movie *Cujo* a lot—and she did *not* have that. Maybe she should just leave, but she had already taken to Luca, and it would be nice to have another friend—even if she had to get along with Wes.

He closed the door and flicked off the light. "Look, I'm sorry I said you had rabies. It's just I don't know you, and this whole situation is extremely out there. Like a whole other fae world out there."

Pursing her lips, Bray pulled at the edge of her braid in the dark. "It's okay." She understood that most humans would have acted worse than Wes had—maybe.

"Please don't bite me, though."

Right when she thought he might be okay. Frowning, she said as patiently as she could, "I don't drink blood."

"That's a good thing." Pulling back the covers, he slipped his legs underneath, and the mattress dipped beneath Bray. The AC blew hard directly on top of her, and she shivered against its coldness, causing a small sound to rumble out from her mouth.

Laborious breaths were already escaping Wes's lips, so she snuck up to his shoulder while he slept. Bray didn't care that she wasn't sure if she liked him—she curled up against the warmth of his neck anyway, and the heat helped her fall fast asleep.

Five

Brenik
Present Day, 1995

Leaving the tree—*their home*—Brenik flew away from it—

and *her*. He had left Bray a drawing on a scrap of paper like he always did, because no matter what, she was still his family.

The thoughts, the images, this place, Brenik couldn't bring himself to fathom how he had gotten to this point over the years. His head was a place he could not escape—an internal battle with no end. It wasn't her—it was *never* her—it was always him. Brenik got that, but it didn't stop it. Nothing did.

Brenik soared higher and higher through the air as the wind scuffed against his wings. Instead of giving him contentment, it only reminded him of what he was—what he didn't want to be: a minuscule pathetic specimen of existence.

It didn't take him long to reach his destination. The large stone shaped like a rose reflected and highlighted almost a pure white coloring underneath the rays shooting out from between the bloated clouds.

What would make today different from all the other times he had gone there, begged and pleaded to a piece of rock who wouldn't listen to take him back—to end his suffering? *Again, pathetic.*

Brenik landed between the folds of the Stone, remembering how ten years ago he didn't think anything could get worse, but it had.

"Can you hear me?" he asked the Stone of Desire who was either asleep or just didn't give a fuck—the Stone didn't stir. Brenik knew it heard him—it always did.

Slamming his hand against the grained particles, Brenik yelled, "Please, send me home or give me a gift like Brayora's. This is not fair, and you know it."

The first time he had come back was after Ruth died. She may not have been able to provide everything he yearned for, but she had given him attention and what almost amounted to favoritism—the opposite of Junah. It wasn't that Ruth didn't love Bray, she truly did, but he didn't have to compete as hard. Bray never had to be the best at anything, but he did—and it always made him feel inadequate.

"Do you want me to get on my fucking knees and beg? Because I will." Brenik's dark hair swung forward as he dropped to his knees, placing his forearms against the Stone. With a frustrated sigh, he finally let his head strike the hard exterior, and he groaned from the slight ache.

Closing his eyes tightly, tears snuck their way out and rained down in between the folds of the Stone. He had only cried a couple of times in his life, and he couldn't control it now. Barely able to contain himself, Brenik flipped his head to the side, plummeting into a spell of depression as his chest rose and fell inconsistently.

Ruth had already been decaying when Brenik arrived to Earth, and he couldn't—*he wouldn't*—watch himself wither away like that. He was too obsessed by his own beauty and never able to do anything of use with it.

"Please..." he pleaded one more time, rubbing his hand softly against the uneven texture.

The thunder of emotions spewing out from inside him came

to a halt when a shuffling movement caused his body to tremble. But then nothing happened. It was as if it were all in his imagination, until the Stone ruptured, rising from the ground like a volcano, sprouting the alabaster arms and legs. Brenik leaped back as the head shot forward—exactly the same as before: no mouth or nose, only those eyes that could see all. It was as if no time had passed.

"What do you desire most?" the loud voice bounced around inside Brenik's head, rough and laced with fury.

An urge of desperation and sadness lingered, but he wasn't afraid. Brenik rose to full height and rubbed the wetness from his face as the bald head of the Stone edged closer. "I want to go home or have the same gift as Brayora."

Cocking its head, the Stone's black eyes bored into Brenik's, but he couldn't tell what the creature was thinking. "That is impossible."

"Nothing is impossible," Brenik countered, stepping closer to the face that made his life pure hell.

"The paths to crossover worlds will not occur again until one final time which is already set. A special man will open those doors," the voice boomed.

Brenik slapped his hand against his leg in frustration. He didn't have time to hear about people who were special. There was already enough of that with his sister. "Then give me the same gift you gave to Brayora—I deserve it."

"You deserve nothing. Your access was granted."

"We didn't even know where we were going!"

"Alive is better than dead," it answered, voice harsh and dangerous.

"I would have to disagree at this point—a twenty-year-old bat hiding in a tree for a year straight is wretched. I would rather be dead than to continue living like this."

The Stone of Desire slowly lifted its head before tilting it to the other side, eyes seemed to narrow even without eyelids moving. "There is one other option."

"I will take it." Brenik would accept any option at this point in his life.

"You do not know the consequences of your choices," it warned.

"What are they, then?"

"Your heart tells me you want to stay young forever, yet also become human. That is an impossible creation. You can appear human but never be one. With this choice, a hunger will stir inside you after every so many turns of the earth. You will have to feed it to keep up with your desire, otherwise, you will wither and fade. But the cravings will darken your soul—your heart—more than the envy already has. It will all be insatiable—do you accept this?"

The Stone was wrong—he could control anything.

Falling to his knees, Brenik clasped his hands tightly together. "Appearing human is all I need—I accept this glorious offer you have provided, and I'm willing to do what has to be done to maintain it." Brenik didn't really think about his decision. He only knew he wanted it.

"Your choice… Regrets are unacceptable, and a reversal of your decision is impossible because your desire today overpowers any future wishes." Brenik was fine with that, more than fine.

Slowly, he nodded as the Stone's arm crawled forward. Lifting its hand up over Brenik's entire body, the Stone moved downward, and a shadow that appeared to be crushing Brenik enveloped him completely. The darkness surrounded him for several long seconds, but then the Stone's hand ascended, allowing light to pour in.

Brenik glanced over his shoulder, where he could still see the obsidian wings attached to his back—even his height remained the same. "Nothing is hap—"

An unimaginable blast of pain shot through his veins, tearing against nerves, muscle, and bones. *Crack, crack, crack*—breaking and popping sounded as joints were ripped and moved to new positions.

A raw scream escaped Brenik when he felt a hard tear at his back where his wings attached, as if they were being shredded. He watched a lone wing fall to the grass, followed by his other one. There, they both darkened to dirt that disintegrated and faded into the ground.

His entire body groaned as each limb expanded and lengthened, torso and spine stretched to incredible height. The pain decreased when Brenik became the size of a human—*almost* human.

Flexing his fingers, Brenik smiled down at his new body in relief, fascination, and perfection as the spasms dissipated. "Thank you." He looked up toward the Stone, its face unreadable more than ever.

"Do not thank me. This is your curse to bear, but remember … you chose it." The Stone's hand pulled back underneath its chest, and then slithered closer to where Brenik was hunched over. Its hand fisted something inside—finger by finger the extremities uncurled to reveal a rectangular white square, a blank painting canvas.

"What is it?" Brenik asked as he took a step closer to the enlarged hand.

"It is yours to maintain. With blood. When the urges come, the last drop of blood from a human will need to be added for you to stay as you are. Otherwise you will age and die like everyone around you, but what grows inside you now will make that near impossible."

To age and die was a route Brenik would not take—he chose to reach for the canvas. As soon as his fingers brushed the object, a picture took form on the texture—a face—his face. Straight black hair brushed his shoulders, blue eyes stood out against ivory skin, and a well-built torso wore a black collared shirt. A silver-gray background brought him to life within the portrait.

Brenik looked down at himself, his clothing now matching

that of the portrait—or at least the top portion. The bottom half of himself, not displayed in the painting, was barefoot and wearing gray slacks.

A sudden fire sparked in his body from the inside out. Brenik dropped to the ground, instinctively releasing the canvas. Pain expanded in his head, and he pushed his palms against the sides to try and shove the flames away. The hunger, the thirst, the yearning … his already sharp canine teeth slid down into points—he needed it.

As if it was a natural occurrence, Brenik bit down on the weak spot between his thumb and forefinger, letting crimson rise to the surface. Swiping the blood with the index finger of his other hand, he brought himself closer to the portrait on the ground and pressed the red liquid onto his face in the painting.

The canvas rapidly absorbed the blood, and the pain Brenik had felt was already washing away.

"That is only the start," the Stone whispered, and while it sounded melancholic, there was no misery in Brenik.

Gradually, Brenik reached out for the painting, prepared for pain to accompany his touch, but it didn't. A devious smile crossed his face as the Stone of Desire drew back into its natural rose-shaped form without another word.

Brenik would not take anything for granted any longer—he would do as he wished.

Walking was a much slower way to travel compared to flying, but Brenik soaked up each step he took through the forest. He would not go back home yet—not to Bray—not to that *fucking* tree. There wouldn't be a way for him to shrink down to fit back inside of the trunk anyway.

Just the day before, Bray had asked him, "You will always be here for me, right? I miss Ruth so much. I don't know if I made a mistake bringing us here, but if we hadn't come, we would either be dead or running all the time."

He had wanted to tell her that hiding in a tree wasn't any better, but instead, he told her what was most likely true, "You did the best you could. I will always be here for you just as you will always be here for me." Brenik had squeezed his sister's hand and drew her the note the next morning before he left.

Feeling sorry wasn't something he needed to do anymore—he had to focus on himself. His heart now beat free, as if all the chains had been released—the two that were no longer connected to his back was the greatest relief of all. Besides his tiny size, Brenik's wings had also been a heavy burden that he wouldn't have to deal with anymore. He would eventually return to show his new self to Bray, but that could wait.

Contemplating, he finally decided where to go. There were small cabins on the other side of the forest where humans lived year-round, but others only came for summer or holidays. He just so happened to know which ones would be empty.

Six

Bray

Bray awoke to a feeling of comfort. But when she remembered falling asleep on Wes's warm shoulder the night before, her eyes flicked open. No shoulder in sight. Instead, she was nestled in a blanket that was pulled all the way up to her chin, cocooning her in place—same bed, same bedroom, except Wes was gone.

Suppressing a yawn, Bray tossed off the heavy blanket and zoomed out the open door. She found Luca sitting at the small kitchen table, immersed in reading something while scooping cereal into his mouth … or just milk.

"Are you going to eat the cereal with that milk?"

Luca lifted his head from what appeared to be the morning newspaper.

The little beast is something else.

"After I drink the milk, then I'll start on the cereal portion." He smiled. "It's not soggy enough yet."

Bray landed on the table and walked closer to inspect the circle shapes swirling around in the bowl. "It looks extremely mushy to me."

"Nah, it still has a good five-minute wait." Luca brought another spoonful of milk to his open mouth, giving it a loud slurp.

Something looked different about him today as her eyes roamed his face. "Ah-ha!" She examined his hair and took a step closer. "You parted your hair differently today." His bowl hair was parted on the left side with a lock of it hovering a little past his brow, instead of creased down the middle.

Tossing his head back, Luca gave Bray a big grin. "Yeah, one of the girls at school said it would look cuter parted on the side—you know, like that kid from *Terminator 2* and *Pet Semetary 2*?"

Bray had seen both of those and the predecessors, but she was more concerned about the actor. "So, this kid only gets to be in sequels?"

Luca set down his spoon in his bowl, making a loud clank. "No, he was also in *Brainscan*."

That was an odd name for a movie. "Never heard of that one. Anyway, you shouldn't be changing your hair to please other people." Even though his hair did look much better—he might be able to pass for eight now.

"The times are a-changing." Luca beamed as he took his last drink of spooned milk and started on the squishy cereal. "Oh, I also picked you something this morning." He pointed to a beautiful peach on the linoleum counter.

"Yum! You know how to make a bat extremely happy." Bray flew to the counter and took a few bites of the extra juicy peach.

She lifted her mouth from her breakfast and swiped away the juice trailing down her chin. "Where is your brother?"

With his spoon in hand, Luca tipped it in the direction of the back door. "He's outside already, trying to get a little more of the garden finished."

Bray shrugged and returned to eating the peach, while Luca finished his cereal and got ready for school.

After burying her teeth in for one more delicious bite, Bray watched as Luca grabbed his school bag off the back of his chair. "I gotta go to school now, but I'll see you after."

"Okay, but let me follow you outside and check to see if Brenik is here. He probably hasn't come back, though." It had only been one day since her brother had been gone, and she hadn't had a lot of time to worry or miss him after she stumbled upon Luca. Her feelings would change later when she had more time to think.

Once outside, Luca told Wes goodbye, who in turn asked if Luca needed to be driven to school.

Luca answered by doing a weird tilting of the head to make his bangs cover his eye. "I got this, Wes."

Wes responded by scrunching up his face and observing the new hair. "You definitely do, Lu."

Bray flapped her wings and flew up and into her tree hole, scanning the area. No, Brenik hadn't returned—his hammock was propped in the same position it had been in the day before.

A trickle of low grunts came from outside the trunk. Bray peeked her head out to watch Wes as he pounded at the hardened earth with the shovel.

"Do you need some help?" Bray yelled from the hole, smiling.

Wes angled his head to where she was. "What?" he called back, the first word he had given her all morning.

Groaning, Bray pushed herself to stand, hopped up and over the ledge, and flew toward Wes's face.

He didn't seem fazed by her this time—instead he looked more bored than anything.

"No rabies questions today?" she asked with sarcasm and headed for the birdbath.

Puckering his lips, Wes went back to beating at the soil. "Pass." Another one-word answer.

"I can help—if you really need me to."

Halting his movements, Wes turned around to find her perched atop the side of the basin. "I do this sort of thing for a living, you know."

Her brows rose, and she leaned her body to the side to observe his work. "Sure you do."

"What are you, five?" he scolded her and spun back around.

She folded her arms in front of her chest and laughed. "Just remember, I did ask you."

He ignored her after that, but she couldn't help smiling as she watched him. Even though they weren't talking, she still found it more entertaining than sitting in her tree.

Wes left his shirt on today, and it was getting more and more covered in filth and sweat. She wanted to tell him to just take the damn shirt off already.

One by one, he had to rip out most of the small bushes, and even with them looking dead and frail, the roots were grounded deep in the earth.

Wes's muscles bulged, his face reddened against brown skin, and his veins protruded—it looked like his flesh might rip off then produce another beastly form. Bray wouldn't be surprised if that kind of thing happened—she had heard tales of beasts taking other forms in Laith when Junah would tell her and Brenik stories. Needless to say, she didn't ask if he needed any more help, just watched in gratification.

By lunchtime, Wes managed to clear the garden and had a few more flowered plants in place. Wiping sweat from his forehead with his shirt sleeve, he headed inside and came back with keys in hand. Not muttering a single word, he took the truck and drove off.

Bray surveyed her tree hole, then back at the dirt, then toward the open window, before finally letting her gaze linger on the dirt again. An area around one of the rose bushes needed to be patted down a little more, so she decided to head there first.

Stroking the soil with her small hand, she evened out some of the bumpier sections. It reminded her of times in the backyard with Ruth.

"Brenik, I got ya a plastic bag over there. If you want you

can start puttin' leaves in there," Ruth said. "Brayora, you can either help Brenik with the leaves or spread some dirt around."

Bray looked at the pile of leaves that Ruth had raked up. Grinning back at Ruth, Bray dove straight into the mound of leaves.

"I want to do that." Brenik laughed and plopped down beside her, tossing a big leaf at her.

"Leaf fight!" she yelled, and they giggled with each other as they buried themselves deep into the pile.

Ruth strolled up with her hands on her hips. "You two ain't makin' things easy today." She smiled and raked them all up.

Bray looked down at her dirty hands and swiped at the tears with the top of her wrist. She missed those days, but she couldn't turn back time. Some things were impossible.

Since Wes was gone and Luca was at school, Bray decided she needed a bath from all the filth covering her. Brushing as much dirt from her skin as she could, she flew over to the birdbath, and peeped her head over the rim to gaze down at the water. Her lips curled in disgust—birds had already entered her newfound territory. Feathers, bird droppings, and dirt swirled around in the liquid.

"Never mind, bath inside it is," she told herself.

Luca had left his bedroom window partially cracked open, just for her. She dove through it and fluttered her wings past the bathroom until she reached the kitchen area. The black plug in the sink sat directly next to the drain, so she landed in front of it, feet clanking when they tapped the metal of the basin.

With all her strength, she shoved the plug into the hole. Flying back to the bathroom, she found the linen closet open and grabbed a rag.

Darting to the kitchen once more, Bray set down the rag so she could push up the handle of the faucet and shove it to the side for warm water.

Bray pressed down on the soap pump about twenty times too many, leaving brown specks of dirt from her hands on the cream-colored surface.

Bubbles started to spew from the edge of the sink onto the counter, so she hurried to turn off the faucet. After stripping off her clothing, Bray gazed at the water with longing because she hadn't been able to make a bath like this in a while.

She didn't toe her way in, instead, she leaped right into the water and allowed her body to drift to the bottom before springing back up, face covered in bubbles. Bray laughed—she had learned to find ways to entertain herself over the years.

The bubbles died down a fraction, and even though her fingers and feet were already wrinkling, she stayed in the water, floating on her back.

"What are you doing?" a voice rumbled.

Bray gasped, her body jerking. For a moment, she lost the grip on her bat form as her eyes flew open. It was already too late to stop it. Bray's body shook, and every part of her grew and grew—legs lengthened, feet widened, until her limbs pushed her up and out of the sink, tossing her backward on the wide counter.

Bray's eyes trained on Wes's stunned expression, who was staring at her like she was a whole new creature—which Bray guessed to him she was.

The cold air brushed her wet body, and a shiver spread through her. Looking down, she remembered she had no clothing on.

Hastily reaching for the rag behind her, Bray brought it in front of her chest to cover herself, and she could see Wes hadn't moved an inch.

"Um, that isn't covering you," he stated, mouth hanging open.

"I know, you moron, turn around!" she yelled while watching him spin to face the other direction.

Bray focused on her gift from the Stone of Desire. She

hadn't used it in such a long time because of Brenik, and sometimes she managed to forget about it. Concentrating, she let her form shrink back down to her normal size. With quick motions, she dried herself off using the already-wet rag as best as she could, before slipping her clothing back on.

Whirling around, Bray found Wes still facing the other direction, with a hand propped on the wall and his head tilted down. She bet he even had his eyes closed, too. "You can turn around now."

Obeying Bray's command, he pivoted to her, face unreadable.

Cocking her head, she crossed her arms and took a seat on the counter. "Not going to say anything?"

At that moment, his face became readable. "What just happened? I mean, seriously what the fuck?" His hands flew to the sides of his head as he marched up toward her, but then seemed to think better of it and took several steps back.

"What do you mean?" Bray's eyes slid to the side.

"What do you mean, 'what do I mean?' Am I losing my mind here? First, you appeared last night on Luca's shoulder like a damned vampire, then you flew around and talked, and later, you somehow ended up sleeping on my shoulder. Then you went outside and acted like you could work on the garden, which I guess by the looks of it you can! But then you're all swimming around in my sink and then somehow sprouted into a giant." He covered his eyes with his palms before he quickly uncovered them again. "Well, no, not a giant, but a giant compared to what you are now!" Wes threw his hands up in the air and stared at her *very* hard.

Bray was about to explain everything to him, when he started ranting the whole thing over for a second time.

"I did offer to help you in the garden earlier," she pointed out when she finally got a word in. Bray had been willing to shift and become human to help him pull out the old bushes, but *he* was the one who would not cooperate.

Wes took a step forward, blinking, his lips parted in astonishment. "You did offer to help, but not as a full-sized person!"

"Sorry, it slipped my mind." Bray smiled and shimmied to the edge of the counter, swinging her legs up and down.

"Do it again." He inched closer.

"What?" Her head bobbed back and forth between her lap and his face.

"Become full-size," he drawled, a hint of curiosity hidden in his words.

"Why?" she asked, surprised. It *would* be easier to stare him down if she were closer to his height.

"Because it wouldn't feel as weird as talking to a *bat*." Bray didn't understand how it wouldn't feel as weird because she was still the same person, regardless if she was a *bat* or human, but she ignored the way he said the word *bat*.

"Fine," she said curtly and pressed her palms against the counter.

Wes closed his eyes and was in the process of turning around, which she found to be incredibly ridiculous. "What are you doing?"

"I'm going to find you some clothes for when you change into a human." He gave her a look like she should have expected this.

"I don't need new clothing." Bray focused on growing until she sat to full height on top of the counter, hands clenching the linoleum tighter. "See?"

He could now see that her clothes didn't disappear or rip apart, but grew with her. His brows still furrowed. "So, the clothing is magical, too?"

"What? *No.* They are just attached to me, so they grow with me."

"That doesn't add up." He stared at the ceiling, moving his lips as if he was having a silent conversation with himself.

She changed the subject. "Why did you come back so

early?"

He fixed his gaze on her as if she were a real person—which she was. "I had the day off today."

"What do you want to do now?" she asked, rubbing her hands together.

Wes scanned her up and down. "We're going to need to get you some new clothes."

"I have plenty of clothing inside the tree." There was a whole corner in her room stacked with dresses and shirts.

"I should have known you were going to give me an answer like that, but we're still going to at least find you some shoes."

Seven

Brenik

The first time Brenik had learned about Bray's gift was nine years ago at the age of eleven, and finding out had pissed him off.

They were both outside laughing in Ruth's garden, when a large raccoon scurried past them out of nowhere. Bray had screamed so loudly that she frightened her own body to grow into a larger size.

She hadn't just grown, though. Everything about her was human—no pointed ears, no overly sharpened canines, and no wings.

Ruth had been absolutely thrilled when she found out, and Bray quickly learned how to change back and forth between bat and human. Brenik had hated it, hated her for it at first. And he kept thinking that maybe the same thing would happen to him, but it hadn't.

After a while, he accepted what she could do and was grateful for it at times, but a glimmer of envy was always there.

A week after Ruth passed away, adjusting hadn't been easy. Brenik and Bray had both stayed in the hollow of the tree— they had only left to eat peaches—until *that* night.

Bray flew off, and he had known exactly where. Ruth had

talked to her about going to college one day, but Bray always shook her head no, even though the twinkle in her eye told him she wanted to go. *Well, that situation didn't pan out.*

He had decided to follow Bray and caught up to her easily—she hadn't known he was behind her. Just before she arrived in front of the frat house, she descended from the air and ducked behind a car to alter forms to appear human.

Brenik gritted his teeth. How long had she been doing this? Was this her first time? He followed her until she approached a blond guy with a can of beer in his hand.

She had walked right up to him and taken a swig of his drink. "Do you want to go back to a room?"

The blond human licked the center of his lip. "You get straight to the point, don't you?"

"Tonight, I do." Bray's voice sounded different that evening and less optimistic than her usual tone.

Brenik hadn't stayed to hear the rest. He flew back to his tree hole where he had to sit around and do nothing except sleep.

Later that night, Bray had attempted to sneak in, reeking of a mixture of odors he didn't want to think about.

With a scowl, he had sat up. "Why did you do that?"

Startled, she turned to face him. "What?"

"You know what I mean," he fired back. "You went to that party and apparently screwed some guy."

"I did. So what?" she replied, just as bitter. "It wasn't worth it."

"This is wrong, that we had to come here. You can go and do as you please, while the only thing I will ever be able to fuck is my own damn hand," he had growled, beyond fed up.

"It didn't help. It only made it worse," she whispered.

"What do you mean?" Her defeated voice had stripped away his anger.

"I—I thought it would help me feel better and erase some of the pain of Ruth, but it didn't."

"At least you can do anything you want." He would have given everything to be anything other than himself at that moment.

"I know you're frustrated I can become human, but the thing is, I can't be happy about it because I know how much you want it. If I could, I would give the gift to you, Brenik."

She had moved to sit next to him on his hammock, and he wrapped an arm around her waist. "It may sound selfish, but can you not do it anymore—at least for a little while?"

"I don't want to change forms, not after tonight. I promise we'll get through this together and figure something out." He had known she meant it, too.

The next morning, Brenik had drawn Bray a picture in a note, hinting that he would be back in a few weeks. He had flown off in the direction of the Stone of Desire to beg it to do something, so he didn't have to feel like he did—to make it so his sister didn't have to either.

He had pounded over and over on the Stone, but nothing had happened—it chose not to answer him. To try and make himself feel less, he would spend weeks in the forest by himself—completely alone.

Brenik shoved away the memory and attempted to erase it, as he gripped the portrait of himself with a tightened fist to the point where it might rip the material.

He reached the long gravel trail, knowing the cabins weren't that much farther away. The grainy terrain pressed roughly into his feet, but he relished the ache. There would be time for shoes once he got inside.

Crunch, crunch, crunch—a powerful pound to the grainy earth sounded as something—*someone* drew near.

Squinting his eyes against the bright sun to get a better view, Brenik focused intensely on the incoming person. Short black hair shaved close to the head, dark skin, blue running shorts stopping at mid-thigh—no shirt.

Standing his ground, Brenik wasn't going to move around

the guy. The man came to a halt as he approached, causing Brenik to stop in place. He couldn't help but notice the perfectly chiseled chest that seemed to be sculpted from a Greek God itself, and the beads of sweat sprinkled across the guy's forehead and shoulders.

"Are you all right?" the guy asked as he looked Brenik up and down, from his bare feet and back to his face.

"Yes," Brenik responded with a quirked brow. *Why wouldn't I be all right?*

"O—kay. I mean, you're walking around out here wearing no shoes on this rough surface. Not to mention, fancy slacks and a collared shirt." He tapped the tip of his shoe toward Brenik's big toe.

"Just walking back to my house." Brenik pointed in the direction of where the cabins were located up ahead.

"You live out here?" The guy glanced over his shoulder.

"Yeah, cabin twenty-three," Brenik lied with a tone that was comfortable and easy.

"Oh, the Thompson's place. They're back already?"

"No, I'm their nephew, Brenik." The lie slid off his tongue, as if it had been planted and already arranged there.

"Nice to meet you, Brenik. I'm Jeremy Jones. I live at cabin twenty-five year-round." Jeremy stretched out a large hand that was about the same size as Brenik's, his deep brown eyes open and warm.

"You, too." Brenik felt liberated. This was the only other human he had talked to besides Ruth, and he was intrigued.

Jeremy turned around and motioned at Brenik with a wave. "Come on, I'll walk you back since you don't appear to be from around here. No one in their right mind would be walking a track barefoot and carrying around… What is that exactly you're carrying?"

"Oh, just a painting." Brenik drew the portrait closer to his body to protect it, but not because he thought this Jeremy would take it and run. But because it was *his*.

"Right … let me see. My mom's a painter." Jeremy's eyes fixed on the backside of the canvas.

Hesitating for a moment, Brenik finally turned the canvas around to face Jeremy, since it would be odd to try and hide the portrait any longer.

Jeremy let out a low whistle followed by a deep chuckle that made Brenik unable to hold back a close-lipped smile. "So, what I said back there about thinking it strange how you're dressed like this and barefoot"—he looked Brenik up and down—"this just tops the whole cake. Who the hell walks a track like that"—Jeremy tipped his hand down and spun his index finger in a circle—"and then carries a portrait of themselves?"

"It was a gift … from my sister." If Jeremy wanted to know more about his sister, the lies would continue to come easily.

Jeremy inched closer and examined the picture more thoroughly. "She did a damn good job."

"She did." Or at least the Stone had.

They walked for a little longer until they reached the first set of homes. Each one was built from chestnut-colored logs with the same porch steps positioned in the middle where the entrance door was. Jeremy came to a stop in front of cabin number twenty-five. "Well, see you around, Brenik. Take good care of that portrait and make sure the next time I see you, you have shoes on. Who the hell knows what's on the gravel out here."

Grinning, Brenik said, "I'll scavenge some up somewhere."

Jeremy started up the stairs as Brenik turned to head to his new place. "Oh hey, Brenik, do you watch football?"

"I have never watched a game."

"What? That's straight up insanity. My place, tonight at seven. I have the week off, so I'll have plenty of beer."

Brenik had never been into sports much, and every time a game was on, Ruth had changed the channel because no one in the house was interested. He was willing to try new things these days, and Jeremy seemed friendly enough.

It only took him a few minutes to walk the rest of the way to the cabin. The homes were spread out far enough to where there was enough privacy from neighbors, but not too far in case someone was needed in an emergency. But he would be sticking to himself for the most part.

The log cabin wasn't in as great of shape as Jeremy's, but it would do for the time being.

Ascending the couple of steps, each one groaning from the pressure of his feet, Brenik approached the ragged "Welcome Home" doormat. He lifted it by the corner and found the silver key, waiting to be snatched by him.

His stomach rumbled, and he turned back around to the fruit tree in the front yard. Marching back down the steps, he plucked two ripe oranges, his mouth ready for the tangy taste.

Unlocking the door, he headed into his new place—it was the same as the last time he had snuck in there when the Thompsons were gone. They would always leave the windows open, such trustworthy people.

Dust filled his nostrils, and he sneezed inside his inner elbow. Brenik studied his surroundings and recognized the small living room and kitchen. The bathroom and bedroom he remembered were behind the closed door.

He padded into the bedroom and flipped on the light switch—one large bed and a dresser with a mirror on top. His image from the mirror stared back at him. Brenik approached it, gazing at himself—he admired his sleek black hair, pale unlined skin, and the perfect, plump bottom lip. He ran the bottom of his tongue across it as his pale blue eyes watched, and his pants tightened in the area that wanted to be satisfied.

Brenik set the canvas on top of the dresser next to the oval mirror, then walked to lay down on the semi-comfortable bed. Peeling one of the oranges, he took a whiff of the citrusy scent and hunger coursed through his veins, all the way to where his fingers connected to the fruit.

Pulling a fresh slice out, dripping with juice, Brenik placed it between his lips, and savored each magnificent bite. But as the juice and fruit ran down his throat, the orange was no longer sweet—it became bitter and sour before turning to a flavor which had to be similar to decay.

Jolting up from the bed, Brenik ran to the bathroom and gagged over the toilet bowl as he firmly gripped the sides. The fruit started to come back up—it skated up his throat and plunked down into the water, no longer orange but dark and tarnished.

Everything that came up was black as it swirled in the water. Hastily, Brenik flushed the toilet and hurried to lay back down in bed.

Thoughts churned around inside his head of his deal with the Stone of Desire. *So, I won't be able to eat fruit anymore.* There could only be one thing that would satisfy his hunger, and he would do anything to achieve it.

Drifting off to sleep, Bray entered his dreams, even then he couldn't rid his mind of his family.

Brenik fell to the ground in a puddle of goo, two hands gripping his sides to pull him up.

"I cannot be a mother to you both—there was never supposed to be two, not even one. And you're too weak." Bright cerulean eyes stared down at Brenik. "I never wanted this—never wanted to be a mother."

If it was not his mother who was holding him, then who was it? His heavy head lolled to the side, where he focused on another tiny frame holding him, covered in wetness.

"It does not take long for our kind to take care of ourselves, so I know you two can do it. I am sorry, but I cannot stay. As brother and sister, at least you will have each other." Without any tears falling from her face, Brenik's mother flew away. He watched her dark wings beat back and forth as she strayed farther away from him into the distance.

"Little brother," the one holding him whispered in his ear,

while clasping his hands.

Brenik did not say anything—he could not. His body was too weak.

"Brenik, we were together inside our mother. I am Brayora, remember?"

He remembered now as everything came together. Inside their mother, they were able to communicate with each other in different ways. They had given each other names and would listen to their mother's voice and movements.

"I remember," he finally answered.

"We have to leave and find something to eat," she rushed out.

They didn't fight over food inside of their mother's stomach—he had given a lot to Brayora because she was so hungry, even though she had always offered the nutrients to him first.

As soon as Brenik tried to stand from the grassy area, his knees buckled, and he fell back down to the ground.

Brayora grabbed under his arms and dragged him backward, with the energy she must have received from their mother's food. He didn't have the strength to try to do anything on his own.

His gaze latched onto his surroundings and instinct let him know what the various shapes and figures were as he looked around. Brayora halted in front of a tree and slowly lay Brenik's body against the warm dirt.

Wings crinkled behind his back, and he had to adjust them since they were still covered in liquid. The twins needed to find somewhere to wash off.

A boisterous stomping sounded in the distance, and Brenik and Brayora froze. Over the roaring noise, Brenik turned around to see the tree had a small opening on the bottom. "In here." Frantically, he pointed to the hole and motioned Brayora to go inside first.

Gathering as much strength as he could muster, he crawled

inside after her. Brenik swiveled to the side and planted himself against the inside of the tree.

The stomping became louder, and Brenik and Brayora held their breathing steady as best they could.

And then the world turned quiet

Brenik perked an ear up and heard not a single sound—no movement. He believed them to have stopped. Growing braver, he peered out of the hole and squirmed forward. Nothing was there.

"You can come, Brayora." As soon as he scooted all the way out into the light, something snatched him off the ground. Brayora screamed from below and tried to fly up to him, but she could not use her wings yet.

With his heart frantically beating in his chest, Brenik turned to face what had him in their grip. He saw horns—all four black. Two protruded from the front and two from the sides. A flat nose, with thin twin slits, puffed hot air onto his face from a large gray head.

His own body shook with fear as the gray creature pulled him even closer.

"Bat," the creature murmured.

"Yes, that is what I am!" Brenik spat. He was not going to be afraid.

"Feisty, feisty, little bat."

"Let my brother go!" Somehow, Brayora had managed to use her wings and was in front of the horned creature's face.

"Two of you. You are lucky I'm the one who has stumbled upon you."

"Why is that?" Brayora asked as she tried to unwrap the creature's thick fingers from around Brenik's body.

"Because I am one of the only jovkins who chooses not to hunt your kind down." As Brenik got a better look, he noticed the jovkin was female. Her golden yellow eyes narrowed at them, as if she wanted to change her mind and have them for a snack.

Reaching with her other hand, she plucked a luscious peach from the tree branch. "You see this?"

"Yes," Brenik and Brayora said simultaneously. He licked at his lips as the jovkin held the fruit.

"Your kind has been eating all our peaches." Large crooked teeth smiled at the both of them.

"I am sure there is plenty to go around," Brayora insisted.

"That is likely not true, since we eat most of them." The jovkin pushed the peach closer to Brayora, and without hesitation, his sister bit into it. "My name is Junah."

Rotating the fruit toward Brenik's face, Junah brought it up closer to his mouth. It took him four times to finally get a full bite into his small mouth, and the peach was delicious.

After swallowing, he pointed from himself to his sister. "My name is Brenik, and this is my sister—Brayora."

"Where is your mother?" Junah scanned the trees of the forest, searching for what was not there.

"She left because she did not want us," he answered.

The jovkin's shoulders relaxed, then her nose wrinkled in revulsion. "I suppose that means I will have to give you two a bath and find you some clothing. You cannot go around smelling like your mother any longer."

"Can I sit on you?" Brayora squealed as she dove forward to rest on Junah's broad shoulder.

Junah's revulsion subsided, and a glimpse of a smile crossed her face when she brought Brenik to rest on top of her other shoulder.

Brenik was thankful for this because while Brayora's wings were already working, he was still too tired to try his out for the first time.

As she carried them along to the river, Junah's eyes seemed to remain watchful around the area, protective. For the first time in his short life, Brenik now felt safe and secure with his new family.

Eight

Bray

"Hop on board." Wes patted his back.

Bray narrowed her eyes at what Wes was offering her. A moment ago, he had opened the car door for her and was now facing the store, slightly hunched forward for her to hop on his back. He was freshly clean after his shower and wearing a black fitted T-shirt and shorts. "I can walk. In fact, I walked barefoot to your car from the house earlier."

Huffing, Wes turned around to face her. "The fact that you don't care about protecting your assets is terrible. I'm not going to risk you getting tetanus, then have to take you to the hospital and explain this whole strange situation to them. So, hop on." He gestured again at his back.

"This isn't *Pretty Woman*," Bray said as she leaped onto him like a monkey, arms wrapping around his throat.

"It sure as hell isn't—you're at the dollar store, nothing fancy," he coughed out, and she loosened her grip around his throat. "Although, with this getup you have on, all bets are off on what the cashier will be thinking."

"There's nothing wrong with my outfit." It was a halter dress that left it easy for her wings to sprout back and forth—maybe a bit short on the length.

He didn't respond as he gripped her thighs and headed into the store. No one else seemed to be inside besides the cashier.

"Do you have any flip-flops?" Wes asked the cashier at the front.

The gray-haired lady was possibly in her sixties and smacked her gum ever so slowly as she stared at them for a moment. "Yeah. Straight back."

Wes gave the woman a brief nod and carried Bray through an aisle cluttered with a whole lot of candy. She extended her hand to grab a pack of gummy worms, and Wes dodged her to the side, putting the chewy riches out of reach. "Priorities first," he grumbled.

Bray sighed against the back of his neck.

When they reached a large metal basket brimming with shoes, there wasn't much of a selection—black, green, or red. "Where's the pink?" Bray didn't mind the other colors, but pink would have been nice.

"For that, we'll have to move up from dollar territory to Walmart another day. Here, try these on." He snatched a green pair of flip-flops attached together and slipped one on her right foot, then carefully lowered her to the tiled floor.

Bray slid on the other one, and the shoes fit perfectly. Wes knelt and pulled off the tab holding them together. She did a little jog in place to test the flip-flops out, and they felt great.

"They aren't jogging shoes." His gaze shifted back and forth between her eyes and mouth, but a small smile started to tug at the edge of his lips.

"You never know what you might need them for."

"Right, but apparently you can just change, and you know—flutter away." He trickled his fingers across the air like they were running.

Bray tilted her head forward. "Precisely."

Rolling his eyes, he turned around to head back down the candy aisle and snatched the pack of gummy worms as he kept on walking. She plucked a pack of gummy bears and ran up next to Wes, handing him the candy. "These are for Luca."

He didn't answer but grabbed those, too, before turning down another aisle filled with craft items and makeup.

"What are you looking for?" Bray asked curiously as she scanned the area with him.

"Feathers, but they have to be red," Wes responded as he continued his search.

Farther down the row, Bray spotted several packs of different colored feathers—the options were black, green, and red. *Are these the only three colors this store likes to sell?*

Hopping in place, Bray picked up a pack of the red feathers. "Found them! What do I win?"

"Is that a serious question?" Wes started for her and took the pack of feathers from her hand.

"It could be." No one was ever too old for games. She missed playing those.

"I guess those flip-flops are your prize." He smiled and leaned down to snag all four other packs from the shelf—they didn't come with many feathers inside.

"What are you doing with these feathers?" Bray leaned over Wes as he hunched down to search through the area.

Craning his head over his shoulder, he stared at her. "You don't have to get all up in my business, scoot back a little." She moved back maybe a centimeter. Shaking his head, he turned back around. "Luca needs red feathers for his Halloween costume."

"Oh yeah? What is he going to be? Wait, don't tell me, let me guess." She loved to guess things. "A chicken?"

Gazing down at the five packs of feathers in his hands, Wes let out what might have been a laugh. "We'd probably need a hundred more packs of these if Luca was going to be a *red* chicken. But seriously, he's going to be Rufio."

"Who's that?" She had never heard of this Rufio before.

"So, you know *Pretty Woman* but not *Hook*? What world are you living in? You know..." He took a brief pause. "Rufi-ooooooooooo!"

"No." Bray giggled. It was the most enthusiastic she had seen Wes all day.

He rubbed the back of his neck, turning his face, cheeks a little heated. "Well, then it was ridiculous to have done *that*. We have the movie at home, and I'm sure Luca will play it tonight if you ask him."

"Now I definitely have to watch it." Bray's heart fluttered and excitement coursed through her, not only for watching a movie, but getting to see one with her new little beast friend— and maybe Wes.

At the checkout area, Bray propped her leg up on the counter, so the cashier could scan the sticker price tag on the bottom of her flip-flop.

"You could have just taken the tag off and handed it to her," Wes said, silently mouthing to the cashier that he was sorry.

After getting in the car and driving out of the parking lot, Wes looked down at his watch and frowned at the time. "We can get you some clothes later today—I have to pick up Luca. Do you want me to drop you off on the way, or do you want to wait in the car with me?"

"I'll come! I've never picked anyone up from school before. It sounds fun." And she could listen to music in the car while they waited.

"I think you're the only person in the entire world who would say waiting in the pickup line at a school is a fun time."

Something in Bray's chest swelled because he referred to her as a person. "I thought Luca walked home from school."

"He does most days, but he still *allows* me to pick him up twice during the week." Bray thought the bond between Wes and Luca was incredibly sweet and genuine. She wished again that she still had something like that with Brenik, but she shrugged off the negativity. One day there would be—nothing between them could ever truly be broken. He was her little brother, and she would always be there for him.

Wes pulled up to the brick building of the school, and they were already the first one in line. He was about to turn off the engine but paused. "I normally shut the car off, but I can leave it on for you if you want."

"It's not hot, and you forget I do live in a hole inside a tree—no AC in there." She smiled and rolled down her window. "But leave the music on, please."

Wes shut off the car and left the radio on as requested, then cranked down his window. Turning to her, he asked, "So tell me about your brother. Can he become human, too?"

Cringing, she rested her head against the seat and stared at the roof. "He's actually my twin, but he cannot become human—he never quite learned how to cope with that."

"Why?"

She thought about her answer, trying to put herself in Brenik's wings. "I was the only one granted the gift from the Stone of Desire. And since it's just the two of us, I'm the only one who has been around him for the past ten years on Earth—besides Ruth, who found us when we crossed over. Junah took care of us back in Laith for the other ten years. So, I think he feels restricted."

"Can't you just go and hang out with other … bats?" He scratched the side of his head, not looking at her, as if it was hard to say the word and not associate it with the earthling animal.

"No, it's only us here—most of our kind became endangered back in Laith."

"You appear normal from the outside," Wes ventured, "so you could do pretty much anything you want to, right?"

Staring down at her hands, Bray thought about it. "No. No, I can't. I can't because of Brenik. It isn't fair for him, so it shouldn't be fair for me."

"That's a bunch of bullshit. He should be happy that at least one of you can change, instead of just staying cooped up in a hole all day." He gritted his teeth, appearing bothered by the whole thing.

"But he cannot mate," Bray said, her voice serious with an expression to match.

One of his brown brows slid up, arching so high, it disappeared under his hairline. "What?"

"He cannot have intercourse with anyone."

Wes shook his head. "I know what mating is, but I don't understand. Wait … *oh* … because *you* can." He turned to the rolled down window, set his arm on the ledge, and stared outside like it was the most interesting sort of scenery. Talking to the outside, he said, "That's still not a reason to, you know, force you to stay that way." He faced her, then.

"My brother didn't force me. I just told him I wouldn't change anymore." Maybe it should have bothered her, yet it didn't.

"But you offered to help me today with the gardening, and you said after the fact that you were going to change," Wes pointed out. That's true. She would have changed.

"You did look like you really needed the help." A familiar tune came through the car speakers, the voice raspy and alluring, the instruments slow and beautiful. "Oh, this is a good song!" She sang along with the lyrics, letting the beats drift all the way down to her bones.

Chuckling, Wes's shoulders relaxed as his fingers drummed against the steering wheel. Bray listened to the music as they talked for a while longer, until the bell rang from inside the school.

"Let me hide in the back," she said hurriedly. Before Wes could respond, she opened the car door and hopped in the backseat, crashing to the floor.

"Really?" Wes peered over the seat and down at her.

She gazed up at his face, noticing a pale scar above the left side of his lip. "Shh! You're going to ruin the surprise."

"I don't know. Luca's pretty tricky to surprise," Wes said but put on his best poker face as he turned back around.

Bray heard the car door handle lift and open—she shot up as soon as Luca told Wes "hey."

"Surprise!" she shouted, hands banging into the roof.

A scream escaped Luca's throat, and Wes chuckled, a deep rumble coming out between his lips.

Luca leaned around the seat, brows all the way up, hair dangling over his eye, and Bray couldn't stop laughing. "What? How?" he asked, grinning widely.

"I'll explain it all to you when we get back," she answered as she crawled from the floormat and sat in the middle of the backseat.

At the house, Bray told Luca the same story she had told Wes, except leaving out the whole mating situation. She wasn't going to be the one to tell Luca about all that, and she was sure Wes didn't want her to discuss it with him either.

Wes returned outside to grab the bag from the dollar store out of the trunk of his car. He wiped his shoes on the doormat and tossed the feathers and gummy bears onto Luca's lap, before dropping the gummy worms onto Bray's. She had somehow forgotten about those, but immediately tore open the bag and plopped one into her mouth, chewing the squishy object slowly.

"Thanks, Wes. These will be perfect to go with the rest of my costume." Luca beamed, holding up the feathers, and his excited smile made Bray remember Halloween was only a few days away. Bray normally had spent the holiday with Brenik while Ruth passed out candy. Ruth would sew them outfits each year, and even as they got older, they continued the tradition. But not this year, or any in the future.

"No problem, Lu. You know"—Wes's head whipped to the side to face Bray—"she's never seen *Hook*."

"*What?*" Luca screeched, hands flying in the air and slamming down on the couch. "How is this possible? I let it slide with *Brainscan* this morning because that isn't as well known, but *Hook*? I'm turning it on right now. Is that okay, Wes?" He was already digging through a cardboard box of VHS tapes beside the TV, until he found the one he was looking for.

Luca came back, shoving the picture on a VHS box in her face. "She looks like you, only with different wings." He pointed to a picture of a fairy on the cover.

"What?" Wes laughed and grabbed the box from Luca. "Are you kidding me? Bray's hair is long and black, she has blue eyes, and her skin is the palest I've ever seen."

Ripping the box back out of Wes's hand, Luca said, "To each their own. Our opinions differ in this case." Luca turned to face Bray as Wes strolled into the kitchen to start cooking dinner. "Anyway, it's like a *Peter Pan* retelling, only Peter is old."

"If it's *Peter Pan*, then I'll watch it." She smiled and bumped her shoulder against Luca's.

Nine

Brenik

Why do I have to feel like this? Brenik thought when he woke from his sleep. There was something inside him that caused him to feel this way. He loved his sister and knew things would have been different if their mother had stayed for them—for him. But she didn't.

Bray had always been there, even when he hadn't wanted her to be. Maybe one day he would realize how thankful he was for her and finally let the jealousy cease to exist. It had already started to wane after the Stone's gift to him.

Pushing away the covers to sit up on the edge of the bed, Brenik rubbed a hand down his still-tired face. He got up to search the room for a pair of shoes, but found nothing, only a wristwatch inside the top drawer of the dresser. It was already six-forty.

He wasn't sure if he wanted to see anyone at the moment, but that was the old Brenik trying to get inside his head: the loner—the wanderer—the outsider.

Admiring himself in the oval mirror, Brenik appeared perfect, except for the wrinkles in his shirt from sleeping. He glided his hands down his face one more time, appreciatively feeling the smoothness of his skin. Before he left for Jeremy's, he glanced at the portrait of himself and smiled.

"I see you didn't find any shoes." Jeremy laughed as he opened the door wider for Brenik to enter.

"Too lazy to put them on. Maybe I'll borrow some of yours later." Jeremy's own feet were also bare, and they looked to be about the same size as Brenik's.

"Depends on which pair." Laughing even louder than before, Jeremy waved him in to where the couch was. "Here, sit down, the game's about to start. I'll grab us a couple of beers."

Brenik sat on the warm cushions of the leather couch. They crunched and squeaked with each movement, and he found the noise exasperating. Along the walls hung old license plates and vintage car posters.

"Here you go," Jeremy said as he popped off the lid and handed Brenik the cold glass bottle.

"Thanks." Gripping the bottle tightly, Brenik sipped the cool liquid and found the taste inadequate. Maybe later he would ask for something stronger. That time didn't come because after a few moments, he immediately regretted drinking anything. "Bathroom?" he asked in a rush.

"Over there." Jeremy pointed in the direction of where it was. Brenik shot for the door, throwing it closed behind him. He had forgotten about earlier with the orange—when the black liquid had bubbled up his throat, slow as a snake slithering out.

The beer didn't come out as liquid either, but made a soft plopping sound as the solid thing thumped into the water—the inky black object the size of a worm.

"You all right in there?" Jeremy knocked on the door with worry in his voice.

No. Brenik knew he wasn't all right. "Yeah, the beer didn't sit well with my stomach."

"From one sip?" Jeremy asked incredulously.

"Yes!" Brenik snapped, not meaning to.

"There's mouthwash in there if you want to use it."

"Okay." Turning toward the sink, Brenik noticed the bottle of green mouthwash and the stack of paper cups resting beside it. Hesitantly, he lifted his head from the toilet and stood to grab the bottle.

Pouring the liquid into his mouth, Brenik swished it a few times before hurrying to spit it out, not wanting to vomit up anything else black and solid.

After taking deep breaths to calm himself, he exited the bathroom and found Jeremy already seated on the couch. His legs were spread wide open, with the beer propped in his hand against his thigh, while he intensely watching the game.

"Do you want something else to drink since you can't hold your beer?" Jeremy chuckled lowly as his ebony brows shot up, then his lips puckered, causing Brenik to stare directly at those well-formed lips.

He knew at that moment exactly what he was thirsty for, the episode with the beer already forgotten. "Maybe in a bit," Brenik said, confident enough that there wouldn't be any time for drinking.

"No problem," Jeremy responded, with his gaze glued on the TV.

As Brenik strolled to the couch, a light flutter drifted through his entire body. The gentle sensation pulsated more and more until a growing intensity took its place when he sank down next to Jeremy.

Jeremy didn't seem to notice that Brenik inched closer, his arm practically brushing the dark flesh of Jeremy's arm. Their skin was like night and day next to each other—the perfect yin to the yang.

The saliva inside Brenik's mouth built up from the craving

beating against his taste buds and intestines.

Brenik had no idea what was going on with the football game because all he could focus on was the growing bulge that now throbbed against his pants.

With not a care except to get what he wanted, Brenik leaned forward and gingerly pulled the bottle out of Jeremy's hand, then placed it on the wooden table in front of them. "I think I'm thirsty now," he said, flirtatiousness enveloping each and every word in the short sentence.

Jeremy scanned Brenik's expression for a second, appearing confused. A look of realization worked its way onto Jeremy's face and he leaped up from the couch. He took several steps back, holding his hands up defensively. "Whoa! Hey, man, I don't swing that way. I mean, it's cool if you do, but I don't."

Brenik could hear the false sincerity of those words, and he could smell the desire that radiated from Jeremy. The bulge in Jeremy's pants seemed to grow as Brenik swiped his tongue across his lower lip and stepped closer to him.

"Are you sure?" Brenik asked as he moved forward enough to where they were practically touching. If Jeremy's answer was yes, then he would turn around and leave.

"No?" A question in his answer gave Brenik all the incentive he needed. He edged forward, chest touching chest, and backed Jeremy up into the wood-paneled wall. They stared at each other for a moment before Brenik crashed his mouth against Jeremy's. Jeremy pulled Brenik's head closer and opened his mouth to him, and they moved their lips back and forth against each other, deepening the kiss as far as it could get—their tongues tasting one another.

The taste wasn't what he craved, though—Brenik needed more. "Turn around," he instructed.

"You want me to turn around?" Jeremy leaned back, eyes filled with desire, knowing good and well what Brenik wanted.

"I said turn around," he commanded.

As if he was in a hurry, Jeremy faced the other direction. Brenik pressed firmly against him from behind, his breath striking the male's warm neck. He tugged Jeremy's shirt over his head, tossing it to the floor, before licking his way up the male's salty skin from shoulder, to neck, then to right under his jaw.

A low growl escaped Jeremy's throat as Brenik slid his arms around the male's sides to his defined abs, and straight to his pants. Unzipping Jeremy's zipper with a slowness that teased them both, Brenik reached in and pulled him out, taking his large size in his hand.

Brenik may have never done this to anyone else before, but he had done it so many times to himself that he was a master at it. He stroked Jeremy up and down while tightening his grip and rubbing his own self against the male's backside.

It didn't take long before release hit Jeremy, a deep groan spilling out from his lips. Brenik ignored Jeremy's pleasured state, feeling unfulfilled—it wasn't enough for him—he needed a different sort of release to conquer the one inside his pants.

The smell of Jeremy's neck and the increased pulse in that lovely thin vein called out to Brenik. A natural instinct stirred inside him, his canine teeth tingling as they lowered. He told himself no at first, but he couldn't control it because he was also telling himself yes. With one quick flick of the head, Brenik buried his teeth deep into the side of Jeremy's neck— the skin easily breaking and opening for him as if it wanted the euphoria, too.

Jeremy let out a cry of pain that withered into a soft moan of ecstasy. The flesh of Jeremy's neck pressed against Brenik's lips as he drank the red liquid, fulfilling him and not fulfilling him at the same time.

He couldn't stop, not even if he wanted to—the metallic flavor intensified everything, lighting him up from the inside out. Jeremy's breaths slowed down, and Brenik needed more.

The breathing from the body ceased, but Brenik didn't finish until the last drop sat on his tongue. Carefully, he lay the body softly on the wood floor and took off for his own cabin. He didn't think about what he had done, only what he needed to do.

When the urges come, the last drop of blood from a human will need to be added for you to stay as you are. The words of the Stone repeated over and over and over and over in Brenik's head as he hurried across the tall grass, finally reaching his cabin.

Not stopping once, Brenik ran through the house toward the bedroom, then placed his finger inside his mouth into the pool of liquid surrounding his tongue. In front of the portrait, Brenik examined it thoroughly and pressed his index finger against his painted face on the canvas.

The blood settled there for several long seconds before becoming engulfed by the portrait, fading bit by bit until there was no crimson left to be seen.

A fullness flowed through his spine, his bones, his muscles, and his skin—as if everything was tightening.

In the mirror's glass, Brenik studied his image, which watched him in return—the same way the portrait did. He appeared fresher, not realizing how tired he had looked before. His pale skin glowed and his hair shined, radiantly.

Jeremy... Hurrying back to the other cabin, he knew what he had done was wrong. Brenik wished there could have been another way, but he hadn't been able to control himself.

The body lay on the floor, looking pale even against Jeremy's dark skin. Tiptoeing forward, Brenik knelt toward Jeremy and kissed his own index and middle finger with a soft press of his mouth. He placed his fingers against Jeremy's dead lips. "Maybe in another lifetime things could have been different." He had to brush away the somber emotion that washed over him.

Brenik needed to figure out how he was going to do this,

how often this situation would occur. Gazing down at Jeremy, Brenik scanned his body, knowing they were the same size. Not fully wanting to, he scrambled around the house, filling a trash bag with clothing, money, and other essentials he would need.

Hate consumed him for what he was doing, but he told himself that Jeremy was dead—there was nothing he could do to change that.

Brenik scurried back to his new home. The other cabins close by were empty, so he wasn't sure how long it would take for Jeremy's body to be discovered.

Without pause, he dropped the bag in the living room and went to the bedroom to sit down, smacking his hands against his face.

"What is *wrong* with me?" Brenik stood up and paced back and forth across the wood flooring of his room, his whole body thumping along with each step. "I hate myself. I love myself. I hate myself. I love myself. It felt good doing it."

"But you feel pitiful now, don't you?" he answered himself, needing to talk to someone. The only person he could talk to would be Bray, but he couldn't tell her what he had done.

Slamming a hand hard against the wall, the sound reverberating, he left a dent. But he didn't feel better, so Brenik did it again and again, his hair bouncing in his face.

"I don't know what I want. I never know what I want. I have what I wanted." Minutes passed as Brenik took in slow breaths, repeatedly trying to calm himself down, until he felt good again. Brenik had no other choice—he would get used to this, then maybe he could figure out a way to do it on the side as he lived a real life.

Blowing out a breath, Brenik walked back into the living room and picked up the trash bag filled with the things from Jeremy's place. He dug his hand around its contents, until he found exactly what he was looking for.

Biting his lip, Brenik pulled out one black dress shoe,

followed by the other one. He slipped both on his feet and stood to full height. Without any shape of a smile, he looked down at his shoed feet. "I knew we were the same size."

Ten

Bray

For the past week, while Wes was at work and Luca was at school, Bray kept herself busy by unpacking moving boxes—since the job wasn't getting finished.

She arranged the movies first in alphabetical order, and when Wes saw what she had done, he gave her a smile and said, "You should have 'consulted' with Luca first. He's going to arrange those from his most treasured to his least favorite."

Bray only puckered her lips at him for that comment. But sure enough, Luca came home and arranged the movies beginning with *Hook*, next came *The Goonies*, and so on. "Goonies Never Say Die," he had said when he placed that one next to *Hook*, then turned around to put the rest up.

The croquet ball was already beside Bray's bare foot, ready to be struck by the mallet when Luca came home, backpack slung over one shoulder.

"Why don't you wear that thing properly over both your shoulders?" Bray asked as Luca shut the gate behind him.

Glancing down at the strap that was missing from his shoulder, Luca brought his head up and smiled. "This is the cool way to wear a backpack."

She didn't see what was so *cool* about not balancing the

weight properly on his back, because she was sure one side of his body would gain more strength versus the other one. *Oh well*, it was his choice after all.

Luca hurried inside the house to set his backpack down while Bray practiced her swing. They had played the game together over the weekend while Wes finished in the garden. That time Wes did remove his shirt, and Bray had to keep her eyes from shifting in that direction. When her thoughts drifted to wondering what he would look like without his pants, she had thought that maybe he should have left the shirt on.

"Okay, I'm ready, and look who's joining us today," Luca called as he stepped outside with Wes.

"You practically forced me," Wes grunted as he picked up a red-striped wooden mallet from the grass.

"You mean, you practically begged me. 'Oh, Luca, you're going to play croquet again?'" Luca said in a deep voice that was strikingly similar to Wes's monotone sound.

"I'm not even going to qualify that as begging, but be prepared to be taken down, Lu." Wes pointed the mallet head at Bray's face. "Bray, I saw your skills over the weekend—you're going to be taken down, too."

"We'll see about that," she said. They were only going to play one round, because Luca had to get ready for Halloween as Rufio. She had already watched *Hook* three times with him, and she found herself quite enjoying it.

With focused precision, Bray eyeballed the space where she wanted to tap her ball to land. She squinted her eyes, lightly hitting it, and the ball moved a couple of inches. She'd thought she had it that time.

Huffing sarcastically, Wes set his mallet against the grass and shuffled toward her. "Let me show you how to properly hit the ball."

She did need a little help—*or*, maybe a lot of help. Croquet wasn't as easy as it looked—only for Luca.

Centering himself behind her, Wes tucked Bray closer to

him until his chest was planted to her back. Well, Bray may have leaned back into him. Either way, she shook off the feeling of his warmth, along with whatever good-smelling scent he was wearing, and positioned herself forward to hit the ball.

"Ready?" he whispered next to her ear.

A tickling sensation filled her stomach as she replied, "I'm ready."

With her hands gripped between his, together they swung the mallet back to strike the ball … and missed. The ball went around the metal loop instead of through it.

"Oh. Come. On!" Luca sighed and hurried over, brushing Wes to the side with the tip of his blue-striped mallet, then dragged the green ball back with it. "I guess it's time for the master to help the lady out."

"I think so too," Bray joked, laughing as she turned to Wes, who was watching them with a genuine smile on his face.

Luca wrapped his gangly arms awkwardly around her, his head somewhere just above her midback. Swinging the mallet backward together, they struck the ball, and it went beautifully through the hole.

Pulling away from her, Luca snapped his fingers and pointed the index ones at Wes, eye partially in a wink. "It takes a master, Wes—only a true master."

A brow drew upward on Wes's forehead. "Let's not get cocky now." He lifted his wrist up to check the time. "Anyway, you better hurry and get ready if you want to go."

"Yes!" Luca said excitedly and rushed inside.

Turning to Bray, Wes said, "I'm still surprised he wants me to go with him. He's getting to that age where he's going to want to do everything with his friends and without me."

Bray doubted that would happen.

"You are a really good brother, yet you're more than that. I've only seen you two together for a short while, but you're his father, his mother, his friend, his disciplinary, and his heart.

It's beautiful." She meant every one of those words.

Wes's face softened. "I think you just made me feel sappier. After our parents died, it was hard at first. We had our grandpa who was able to step in, and I worked part-time with him at his landscaping company while I went to college. When the heart attack hit him, I—I had to drop everything. My focus has only been on Luca—is on Luca." His voice broke, and she caught his eyes becoming glassy. He rubbed a hand against the back of his neck and changed the subject before Bray could respond. "You know you're welcome to come tonight."

She wanted to ask Wes more questions about his life, but instead, she just grinned and started to help put away the croquet set. "Luca is ahead of your game, he already asked me."

Wes dropped the balls in the black bag. "I'm surprised he didn't ask you to dress up, too."

"Oh, he did. He wanted me to be Tinkerbell." Bray laughed.

"You should have told me. I could have picked something up for you."

"I got crafty while I was alone today and made wings with coat hangers and pantyhose." The hanger had taken a while to curve just right, but eventually she accomplished it.

"Where did you find the pantyhose?"

"I have all kinds of treasures in the tree hole." Bray couldn't remember where she had found them. It might have been the garbage, but they had been unopened.

A mixture between a frown and confusion crossed Wes's face. "If you consider that a treasure, I need to get you some better things."

Bray scurried away and climbed up the tree to retrieve the dress for her costume, since she didn't want to morph outside in the open.

She peered down at the ground, finding that Wes had moved closer to the tree, watching her with what may have been a little worry.

"Couldn't forget this." She held the tiny green dress, that she had cut out from fabric earlier, down toward his face. It was much easier for her to make a small dress than a large one.

He arched a brow before she turned and strode for the house.

Once inside, she headed to the bathroom, changed to her bat size, switched clothes, then returned to her human form. *That was easy.*

Bray found the flat shoes by the front door that Wes had gotten her the other day from Walmart—which he had said was a step up from the flip-flops. Then she grabbed the wings from the coffee table, put them both on, and waited for the boys.

Luca strolled into the room with his hair slicked back and a little poof in the front, bags of feathers in hand. "Can you help me with these? I can't put them in right."

The costume almost exactly matched the character in the movie—tight black shirt showing some skin, ripped black pants over red leggings, red shoes, some type of vest with fringe, and a necklace that resembled bones. "You look great, Luca. Now, turn around so I can work on this hair."

Following her instructions, Luca held up the bags of feathers, his hair rock hard from a little too much hairspray.

She lined the feathers down the right side of his head, then moved toward the middle, followed by the left side. "I think we are going to need a little more hairspray to keep them in place."

Carefully, she pulled him in the direction of the bathroom to make sure he didn't move his head. Taking the can of hairspray, she spritzed way more than she probably should have, but at least they were glued into his hair now.

"Perfect," Luca said and softly patted over the feathers. He looked adorable.

They found Wes in the living room, already sitting on the couch in his Captain Hook costume—it didn't resemble the one from *Hook* in the slightest.

"You two are lucky that I even found this at the store. I almost had to go with a Ninja Turtle." Wes rolled his eyes and held up the poorly-made plastic hook.

"It looks great," Luca said. Wes did look great, sexy even, as his uncovered hand stroked the plastic hook.

"Very Hook like." Bray beamed.

Wes and Bray walked up and down the street, watching Luca's bucket fill with candy. Bray snatched several pieces along the way. The night was wonderful, like the Halloween nights her and Brenik spent with Ruth—except this was better.

She loved seeing all the costumes: ghosts, Frankenstein's Monster, Ninja Turtles, Rainbow Brite, the Addams Family, and other ensembles she didn't recognize.

They were at the start of a new street, when a loud boom up ahead signaled into the night. Luca and Bray froze in place, while Wes appeared calm as he pulled Luca back and said, "We need to go home now."

"There was a gunshot," Luca whispered. His eyes became wider when sirens wailed down the street, swiftly passing them by.

Curiosity pulled Bray in the direction of the flashing lights, but she needed to make sure Wes and Luca got home safely.

They rushed down the uneven sidewalk, lights illuminating the already darkened street. Bray had a feeling she should find out what was going on.

When they walked through the front door, Bray held it open and dropped her fake wings to the floor. "I'll be right back." Behind the open door, she transformed herself into her bat form and took off, hearing the voices of Luca and Wes calling after her. But she pushed their voices aside.

She flew high in the air, over the tops of the trees, until she saw the flashing lights of police cars. Some people stood outside houses, while others were trying to get a closer peek at what was happening.

Cops were pushing people away, and Bray craned her neck to get a better view. A body she couldn't see clearly was being covered with a white sheet by a paramedic. Bray landed on the top of a tree and shimmied down to where she could hear a lady ranting to a cop about what had happened. "This man came down the street and suddenly had me on the ground, clawing and then choking me. His face only showed rage— that was all that seemed to exist in him." The redheaded woman's voice quivered as she wrapped her arms around her middle, visibly shaken.

"Then can you tell me what occurred next?" the police officer asked, his face hidden from the darkness.

"My husband tried to knock the man away, but the attacker wouldn't stop. So, my husband got his gun and shot the man. Even after the bullet hit him, his eyes still looked murderous when he was falling to the ground. But I don't understand why there isn't any *blood*—there was none from the wound—only what appeared to be two wounds on the side of his neck with dried blood." The woman shivered as she continued to hold herself.

"The body is going to be taken to the hospital to be examined. We will have more questions later, but this is all I need from you tonight." The officer closed a small notebook in his hand and moved in front of another man to ask further questions.

The only kind of bites on the side of the neck that Bray could think of were those inflicted by vampires, but that was only in the movies. Besides, the lady hadn't mentioned him attempting to bite her in that area. From the way she described what had happened, it sounded like he had a case of rabies, but humans didn't act like that when they got bit by a rabid animal.

The redheaded woman walked back toward an elderly lady with tight gray curls and said, "Thank you so much again for calling the police. They arrived right after Jerold—" She started to sob, and Bray had heard enough.

Quietly, Bray flew back to the house and ran over the story a few times in her head. It did seem strange, but maybe the woman was confused. She had just been through a traumatic experience. Bray didn't know if the lady had gotten close enough to see if there really had been blood or not around the bullet wound either.

As soon as Bray rounded the corner of the street and approached her home, she found Wes waiting on the porch. He was still in his Captain Hook attire but had already taken off the hat and hook. He opened the door for her as she zoomed inside and transformed herself.

"What was that, Bray?" he demanded.

"What do you mean?" she asked. The sound of the running shower echoed from the bathroom, where Luca must be.

"You can't just *do* something like that."

Her eyes narrowed and met Wes's fierce gaze. "I can *do* whatever I want."

"Not if it's going to affect Luca. There was a *gunshot*, Bray. And you just morphed and zipped right off, not letting either one of us know where you went. What if something had happened to you? What if someone saw you?"

"I've been flying in the dark for years, Wes. Even if someone saw me they would probably think I'm an Earth bat."

"No one would believe you were a *bat*," he spat, pulling at the ends of his hair.

Bray took a step toward Wes. "I don't understand what the big deal is." She didn't understand why he was acting like this.

"The big deal is that Luca is already growing attached to you. I don't even know what we're doing here. Are you just going to live with us for the rest of our lives like some little pet?" Wes lifted his hands up and brought them down heavily against his legs, the slap reverberating through the house.

"Is that what you think of me as?" Bray's eyes shifted side to side, fighting back tears.

"If that's what you want to be." He shrugged. She felt like

she had been more than slapped. It was as if her insides had shattered into too many pieces to be put back together. Well, she shoved them together anyway because she felt angry.

"You know what, screw you!" she cried and ran for the door, throwing it open while transforming to fly back to her tree hole. She couldn't believe he would say something like that to her. Bray was no one's pet. Was that all anyone would ever see her as? Was that how Junah and Ruth had seen her and Brenik as—*pets?*

Both hammocks were empty, of course. She looked at Brenik's and wished he was there because at least he knew they were the same—even if she could transform. Hurrying over to his hammock, Bray flipped to her stomach and let the tears fall and stream down her face.

A few moments later, her home shook and the trunk groaned as a shuffling against the tree bark sounded. Bray didn't move, only waited to see who it was. If it was Luca, she would talk to him. If it was Wes, he could piss off as Ruth would have said.

Leaving the comfort of Brenik's lingering scent, Bray sat up in the hammock as it gently swayed. Bray waited. A light came into view and shined directly in her face. She hissed at the brightness, angrily covering her face with a hand.

"Maybe you actually are a vampire." Wes tried to smile as he lowered the beam of light. But more than anything he looked weary.

She needed him to go away. "Not funny. You can go back inside, because I don't want to talk to you ever again."

"Listen, I'm sorry for what I said in there. I didn't mean any of it—I was just pissed and worried. I didn't know what to tell Luca, who had gotten upset. This whole week has been extremely bizarre. Plus, I'm up here whispering to you in a hole inside of a tree. You have no idea how terrified I am of heights." He glanced down. "My hands are shaking."

Her eyes shifted to his hand gripping the flashlight, and he wasn't lying, it was trembling.

"Okay, I forgive you." She may have forgiven him too fast. But even with a fear of heights, he had climbed up there anyway, so the least she could do was forgive him this time. Brenik had said plenty of heated things when he was having one of his moments. She probably had, too.

"That's it? I thought you weren't ever going to talk to me again." Skepticism spread across Wes's face.

"I changed my mind—but just this once." She grinned and stood from the hammock.

"Look, you don't have to tell me where you come and go to. But if you need to go somewhere and Luca is right there, at least let him know. Please?"

"Agreed." Bray understood that Luca was still young and didn't understand everything in the world yet. She didn't either.

As Wes climbed down the tree, Bray flew to his shoulder and told him about what she had seen and heard at the crime scene.

"It definitely does sound like something a rabid dog would do, minus the choking part, but some people in this world are just completely off their rocker." Wes rubbed at his chin as he looked up at the night sky. "The blood thing, though, when you're frightened out of your mind, you don't really pay attention to detail. Who knows what stuff the lady was imagining if her breathing was being cut off."

"Yeah, who knows. I'm sure there isn't anything to worry about." Bray felt like she was lying to herself a little bit, because it still was strange.

"There's someone I think you need to talk to, though," Wes pointed out. Bray knew he was right.

When Wes walked her inside, Bray hopped off his shoulder and transformed.

"Also, warn me about that next time, too," Wes said with sarcasm. Then he headed to the living room without looking back.

The light beamed out from underneath Luca's closed bedroom door. Tapping softly on the wood, Bray took a step back. "Come in," Luca's soft voice answered.

Bray opened the door to find Luca leaning against the headboard of his bed. Wet hair framed his face and a book was flipped open in his hand.

"What are you reading?" Bray asked as she took a few steps closer.

Unsmiling, Luca glanced up at her and then back at his book. "*The Lion, the Witch and the Wardrobe.*"

"I love that book!" That was one of the first stories Ruth had read to her and Brenik. She remembered almost all of it by heart.

"Me, too. It's my favorite out of the Narnia books." Hers, too.

She owed him an apology. "I wanted to say I'm sorry about earlier. I didn't mean to leave like that."

"It's okay. I should be used to people leaving by now—they always do," Luca whispered, not meeting her gaze.

Bray knew that feeling all too well, and tears pricked at her eyes. She didn't want anyone else to feel that way. Especially not the little beast who had become a friend in such a short time.

"If I ever leave to go somewhere, I'll let you know from now on," she promised.

Luca nodded, his face relaxing. "Thanks, Bray." He was about to return to his book, but then he stopped. "Do you want me to read some of the story to you, since you like this book, too?" A tiny smile lifted at the edges of his lips, freckles highlighted under the incandescent light bulb.

"I would love that." She looked at his small twin bed, wrinkled her nose, and switched back to her bat form. Bray flew up to his cozy shoulder and curled into a ball, his soft voice enveloping her through each wonderful word he read.

She had been sleeping in her tree house for the past week, but she could barely keep her eyes open. Luca had gotten to the part where the lion finally made an appearance, and those were the last words she remembered before falling asleep on her friend.

Eleven

Brenik

Brenik had cooped himself up in the house for the last week.

At night he would go for walks around the graveled track, thinking to himself.

Every time he passed by Jeremy's cabin, shame washed over him at what he had done, yet the inevitability of it lessened his self-loathing somehow.

He could not bring himself to check inside the house to see if the body was still there. He was sure it was.

Just like the tree, the cabin had turned into a prison, swallowing every part of him, until he was becoming that thing inside again he despised. Taunting—toying—obsessing. His head was a place he hated to be in almost all the time.

Urging himself to do something, he decided to walk for a while. Crickets were chirping, and he missed his sister. Brenik had spent twenty years around her, so he couldn't help it.

Street lamps slid into view, and the loud music coming from Sam's Bar boomed through the air.

As Brenik drew nearer, he could see the graveled parking lot filled with cars. Through the open windows of the building, the clanking of pool balls smacking each other sounded.

The place itself was a dump. *But what the hell?* He needed

to get away from his old loner self, so he might as well check it out. Shuffling himself between two cars parked too close together, Brenik headed for the glass door at the entrance.

Inside the run-down building, he found himself engulfed in a room full of smoke, loud music, and a cluster of people. His gaze darted around the room, taking in everything. Brenik had been there before at night and peered in, but he had never gone inside. He now wished it had stayed that way—the place was disgusting.

Box TVs, playing different channels, took up each corner of the room, but the sounds were overpowered by the terrible twangy music.

Several guys and girls in the middle of the room, past the four pool tables, were throwing darts at a dartboard. *Playing poorly*, he added to himself, as one of the tall girls in a miniskirt missed and struck the blue painted wall.

Growing bored already, Brenik looked toward the bar area filled with more people. They bounced drunkenly, except for one woman with hair like shadows that fell to her shoulders. She sat alone, gazing down at her drink.

Feeling alone himself, Brenik swaggered over to the bar and took a seat on a torn cushioned stool beside her. The bartender was busily waiting on other people, and after what happened at Jeremy's, he wouldn't be having any alcohol tonight.

Under the hanging lights, Brenik turned and gazed at the profile of the woman's face: warm brown skin, dark brows, a tiny mole a few millimeters below her bottom lip. He felt the urge to lick it, but he didn't.

He continued to study the woman. As if she felt him watching her, which she probably did, her eyes flicked back and forth to the side to see if he was still looking at her—which he was.

She spun her stool abruptly to the side, and asked, "Are you not drinking?"

Brenik stared at her ruby red lips. "Not tonight."

She pulled her drink closer to her, as if she was afraid he was going to drop something in it. "Then why are you up here?"

"I saw you sitting here and thought I'd say hello." He liked that this woman pretended to not seem the slightest bit interested in him. "So, hello."

"Goodbye." She smiled and turned her chair back to face the front.

Leaning forward, he whispered in her ear, "My name is Brenik."

"That's lovely." Still smiling, she brought her drink to her mouth and set it back down on the bar underneath her chest, which he was looking at, but trying not to.

"Your eyes are telling me differently."

"Okay, what kind of line was that?" The woman laughed under her breath. "Shouldn't you maybe move over there?" She pointed in the direction of the stools filled with women in tight dresses at the opposite end of the bar table.

"Sorry, the seats are all taken." He smiled like he had just revealed a secret.

"Then, silence is a must. Shh!" She pulled up an index finger in front of her red-lipstick covered lips. Her eyes seemed to beam, as if she was starting to become entertained.

"So, do you want to come and hang out at my place?" He coughed. The smoke was really starting to mess with him, and he was tired of trying to talk and listen over the music.

Slowly, she swiveled her chair back to face him and arched a brow. "Look, just because you have a semi-pretty face, doesn't mean I'm going to come home with you and hop in your bed."

"Only semi?" He cocked his head, biting his lip.

"Wow. Okay, whatever. I never—and I mean *never*—get hit on and when it finally happens, I get a stalker?"

He shrugged. "I've never had a relationship."

"I highly doubt that." She laughed and brushed a lock of hair away from her face.

"Listen, I was pretty much homeschooled my whole life, so my social skills are not up to par. But I *promise,* you don't have to worry about stalking." He didn't have the drive to sit there and bother with that nonsense.

She stared at him, as if trying to find a way to doubt his story, but what he said was true. Ruth had tried to school them the best way she could, even though he didn't grasp everything she had tried to show him.

"Not everyone is going to break your heart," he added. "I just haven't been around a lot of people, and I want to change that." Brenik held out his hand. "And you are?"

The woman let out a long sigh. "My name's Rana." She gingerly enfolded her hand into his.

"A very exquisite name."

"What *exquisite* vocabulary you have, Brenik." She rolled her eyes but couldn't contain her smile.

"My name did sink in for you, then."

"Maybe it did," she whispered.

Brenik stood from his chair, itching to leave the bar. "So, hang out?"

"I'll come hang out, but only because I'm in a weird place tonight. And—don't even think anything frisky is going to happen, because it isn't, Brenik." Rana grinned and Brenik's stomach fluttered at the sight.

"Anyway, let me call my friend real quick and let her know if I disappear, it's because of some guy at a bar," she teased. Taking her drink with her, Rana went to the end of the bar and picked up the phone, then dropped in a quarter to call her friend.

Brenik looked around the room while he waited for her, still unimpressed with the crowd and décor.

Rana walked back toward him a few moments later—still smiling and appearing genuinely amused. "I described to her exactly what you look like, so be prepared if I go missing.”

Giving her a small smile in return, Brenik said seriously, “Don’t worry, you can leave anytime you want. I’m really not a stalker.” He wouldn’t feed on this woman—there was something about her he was attracted to.

Relieved to be outside, Brenik took in a deep breath of the fresh air. Getting away from the horrific atmosphere made him feel better already. He had no idea what intrigued humans so much about that kind of life—but if they were drunk or high, anything must seem like a good time.

“Where are you parked?” Rana surveyed the graveled lot, waiting for Brenik to point to one of the cars.

“I walked here.” He motioned in the direction he had come from.

“I should have guessed you’d say something along those lines,” she said sarcastically.

“Well, I don’t have a car.” Brenik shrugged as he smiled at her.

“Let me guess—you don’t have a job either?”

“I did say I was homeschooled before. But I’m attempting to become an artist.” He had to make something up. All he could think about was the portrait at the cabin, so an artist was the first thing to come to mind.

“At least you have some kind of goal.” Pulling the keys out of her purse, Rana headed toward an aging silver car.

After he took a seat on the passenger side, she turned to face him. “Wait, how *old* are you? You’re legal, right?”

“I’m twenty. You?”

“You know, you weren’t even supposed to be in that bar. You’re just a baby,” she groaned. “I’m twenty-four.”

“I do like them older.” He scanned her over and liked what he saw even more.

“Whatever.” Rana laughed. “So where do you live?”

Brenik pointed her in the direction of his home up ahead. Because of the hidden cabins, Rana joked she was inclined to believe that maybe tonight was her night to die. But he wouldn't let himself get out of control.

When Rana pulled up to the cabin, she sat in the car for a moment.

"What's wrong?" he asked, not sure what to make of this woman.

Without looking at Brenik, her head fell to the steering wheel. "It's just… Look, like I told you before, I'm only coming here to hang out, not to *do* anything. It's incredibly cliché, but my boyfriend cheated on me with my roommate, who is no longer my roommate. That's the first serious relationship I've ever been in. Growing up, my parents were incredibly strict, until I moved out on my own a few years ago." She lifted her head from the steering wheel to look at him. "Anyway, I don't know why I'm telling you all this, but I'm here right now to *escape*."

Brenik understood the need to escape more than anything. "We'll just head inside and watch some TV, and then you can go home. How does that sound?" Brenik didn't really know her, but it bothered him that she was unhappy.

"It sounds brilliant." A grin spread across her face, and Brenik wanted to brush his thumb right under her lip where her mole was.

The rest of the car ride to his place was comfortable, easy conversation. Something he'd never really experienced before. It was a different sort of pleasure.

Once they walked inside the cabin, he turned on the TV. "What do you want to watch?" To get rid of the static, he straightened out the antenna to get a stronger signal, but the screen was still a little fuzzy.

The main channel that worked was playing an old episode of *Gilligan's Island*. Rana shouted, "Leave it here! I love old television shows." So did Ruth, but she had been around when the original episodes aired.

Brenik took a seat beside Rana on the old cloth couch and

studied how entranced she was with the show. Her eyes sparkled, and she laughed at things Brenik didn't quite understand. Every now and then, he couldn't help but smile from her giddiness.

He had adjusted well to becoming semi-human and losing his wings. It was as if he had never been anything other than what he was now.

After a few episodes, Rana peered down at her watch. "It's getting late. I have to help a friend move her stuff into the apartment tomorrow morning, so I better head out."

A surge of something unfamiliar found its way inside Brenik's chest, and he didn't want her to leave. Yet he still told her it was all right.

"It was interesting meeting you—maybe I'll see you around?" Rana asked.

"Okay." He didn't sound hopeful or optimistic as he stared at the floor, while she stood in the doorway.

He watched her velvety hair bounce against her shoulders as she descended the porch steps. At the last second, she turned around. "Hey, if you're up for it, some of my friends and I are playing charades tomorrow night if you want to come over."

Brenik thought it over for a minute and knew he wanted to go. "Sure." Charades was something he had only seen on TV—it wasn't a game he had played with Bray or Ruth. Something about that made him feel invigorated.

"Great. I'll pick you up around five—or do you want to walk again?" Rana smiled, and it reached all the way up to her caramel eyes, highlighted from the porch light.

"I can walk." He didn't mind walking.

"That means I'll pick you up. See you then, stalker."

Brenik ran a hand across his face and shook his head.

"Right, maybe I shouldn't joke about such a serious subject." She laughed and waved goodbye as she headed to her car.

Brenik shut the door behind him and crashed his back

against the wood, sinking down to the floor. *I have to figure things out*, he thought as he gripped his hair tightly.

The gnawing inside him had begun to stir again, drowning out the goodness of the evening. He knew the lust for blood would take over eventually, and he almost hated admitting to himself that he had liked the rush of pleasure when it had happened the first time.

One thing he did know: this time he didn't want it to happen around Rana. He desperately wished it hadn't happened around Jeremy either.

A few minutes later there was a knock on the door, and he jumped up to answer it. *Maybe Rana had forgotten something.*

He tore the door open to a face that wasn't Rana's. It was a short, bald man wearing a police uniform.

Dread filled Brenik's chest, and he swallowed slowly. "Can I help you?" he asked, his voice sounding ever so calm.

"We just wanted to inform you that the man who lives at cabin twenty-five was shot down earlier this evening."

Brenik's brows furrowed in confusion. "Shot?"

"Yes. We are investigating the incident and need to know if you've seen or heard anything strange going on."

Brenik thought about it for a moment, but he hadn't heard anything. "No, I was just over there a few days ago, watching a football game. Everything seemed fine."

"Okay. Well, thank you for your time, Mr.?"

"Schwartz." That was the first name he could think of.

"Mr. Schwartz, I can't discuss the case, but there have been reports on the news. Have a good evening." The officer turned around and walked back in the direction of Jeremy's.

Brenik shut the door and headed straight for the TV, flipping it to a station that had local news. The damn antenna wasn't working right, so he swiveled the long metal rod back and forth, until he found the sound coming out clear.

"A man was gunned down earlier tonight after he tried to attack a civilian. It is unknown as to what caused him to spiral out of control, but an autopsy is going to be performed. Police have been baffled by the lack of blood surrounding the gunshot wound. The case is still under investigation.”

What? Jeremy's body wasn't found in his home? He was dead when Brenik had left the house. Sinking down into the sofa, Brenik ran a hand through his hair. He didn't know what to think.

Twelve

Bray

*"**B**ray, can ya go outside and pick some peaches from the tree? I want to make a peach pie for you two," Ruth called from the kitchen to Bray, who was in the living room.*

Bray and Brenik were sitting on the table playing checkers. Brenik was in the process of shoving a black checker forward. "Sure, Ruth!" Bray hollered back.

Lifting her gaze to Brenik, she asked, "Do you want to help me?"

"What else do I have to do?" he responded with a moody grunt.

Bray cocked her head and folded her arms. "I suppose you can play checkers for the both of us while I'm outside."

Brenik shot her a glare, then smiled. "I do want the peach pie as soon as possible and not have you poke around out there."

"Whatever," Bray said. She transformed, and Brenik landed on her shoulder.

"You do not understand how much I wish I could transform, too." He sighed. But she did. For years, she had snuck off to the Stone of Desire, begging it to give the gift to Brenik or let them both have it. Every single time she had failed to rouse the

Stone awake to answer her.

At times, Bray was afraid they had imagined everything. Maybe they were really born on Earth and had never met with the Stone of Desire. She knew better than that, though.

Brenik flicked her rounded ear with his tiny fingers, and she swatted him away. He took off for the tree as she grabbed the wicker basket from the back porch.

"Ready, little brother?" She hadn't called him that in a while, but today was a great day.

Chuckling, he zoomed up to the tree, and she stopped at the base of it.

"Ready!" he shouted down, pushing with all his strength against a peach until it plummeted. Lunging forward, Bray caught the fruit and set it into the basket.

"Again." Bray looked up in between the trees to see where he was, but she couldn't find him. A pink and orange peach fell in front of her, and she sprinted forward, catching it and placing her prize into the basket.

"That was a good one." She grinned. "I didn't even see it coming."

They did this several times. Even though they were older now, games still consumed their day—and probably always would.

After the basket was filled to the brim, they headed back inside. Bray set the fruit in between the pie pan and the other ingredients that were sprawled out on the counter.

Taking out two plump peaches, Bray placed one on the counter for Brenik and brought the other up to her mouth. Delicious. She would never grow tired of peaches.

"We need to figure somethin' out, Bray," Ruth said as she sliced up a peach, "whether you want to go to college one day or what."

Brenik stopped biting into his fruit, and Bray took a deep swallow, growing nervous. She would love to be able to do something like that. They had discussed this before, but it just wasn't fair. "I'll think about it." She could think about it, but she knew what her choice would be.

Ruth stared her straight in the eye. "You've been saying you'll think about it for two years. You just turned nineteen. What are you gonna do if somethin' happens to me, huh?"

"Stay in the tree, I guess," Bray replied with a shrug.

Ruth's hands dropped to her hips, knife tucked in hand. "And what if someone chops down that tree?"

"We'll be okay. We have each other." Bray shot Brenik a glance, but he was glowering at the peach without looking up.

"I know but..." Shaking her head, Ruth focused on Brenik. "Come here, tiny prince, I need ya to help me finish cuttin' these. This arthritis is killin' my fingers." Brenik rushed over, giving Ruth a peck on the cheek, and helped her finish preparing the pie.

Bray transformed back to her smaller size and took off into the living room, plopping down on the table to stare at the checker game. Ruth chuckled from the kitchen, and Bray thought maybe one day, somehow, both she and Brenik could be happy.

Brenik and Ruth had joined Bray in the living room, until the timer buzzed, pulling all three of their attention from the TV. "It's ready," Ruth said as she hurried into the kitchen and took out the warm pie. "And it sure smells damn good."

Brenik craned his neck while licking his lips. Bray then closed her eyes and took a huge whiff of the sweetness. Amazing.

A loud crash came from the kitchen and then a bang on the floor. Brenik was the first to find Ruth on the tile clenching her chest, pie scattered across the floor, already planting a dark and tainted memory within Bray.

"Do something, Bray," he cried hysterically, tugging at Ruth's dress sleeve. "I'm too small to lift her."

Hastily, Bray transformed herself and bent down to Ruth, who was still clutching her dress and attempting to speak.

"Ambulance," she rushed out.

Hurrying to the corded phone above the counter, Bray dialed the ambulance. She pretended to be Ruth, told them where to come, and to please hurry. Nervously, she hung up and bent back down to Ruth. She was struggling worse than before Bray made the phone call, her breaths ragged.

"The tree hole," Ruth rasped. "You two have to go to the tree while they're here."

That was the last thing Ruth said before the clenching stopped, her twitching stopped, and her heart stopped. Brenik howled. Bray moaned. She transformed back to her bat form after opening the back door, and they rushed up to their tree together.

Brenik held Bray as she sobbed against his chest. While he held her, tears of his own rained down on her. This was worse than when they left Junah because at least they knew she was still alive, but this—this was different. Ruth was gone.

"Hey," a male voice whispered. Bray's eyelids flickered open to big brown eyes staring down at her.

"I don't want you to make peach pie," she responded and closed her eyes before immediately opening them again. Bray gazed up at Wes and then looked around the large space—a bed, dresser, messy desk with landscape sketches scattered across, and framed musician posters on the walls. She was in Wes's room, but she remembered falling asleep on Luca's shoulder.

A tear slid down her cheek, and she wiped it away. "Sorry, I know I'm not supposed to fall asleep in there." She was resting comfortably in the middle of one of Wes's soft pillows.

"That's not why I moved you. Luca isn't a still sleeper—he tosses and turns the whole night, and I didn't want you to get crushed. Trust me, I know. He's kicked me a few times when we've had to share a bed before."

Wes was sitting up in the bed, studying her, and all she could think about was that stupid memory. Would Ruth have had a heart attack that day if she and Brenik had said no to pie when she'd asked?

"Just so you know, I don't even like peaches, so I won't be making a peach pie anytime soon. Blueberry might be another story." He smiled. Something in his expression hinted that he was trying to make her feel better. She had obviously mentioned more than she should have during her sleep. Bray would never eat another peach pie again, but she would eat a blueberry one.

She bolted up in a flash. "Can we make one today?"

"I don't even know how to make blueberry pie, much less a *pie*," Wes said.

"Did someone say pie?" Luca asked as he strolled into the room, rubbing sleep from his eyes.

"No pie," Wes said with a tone that didn't invite further discussion.

Luca glanced at Bray with a grin. "Two against one," she said, smiling mischievously at Wes.

"*Fine*. I'll buy the ingredients, but you two can do all the work," he said, his voice filled with amusement.

As they all agreed, the three of them went to the store together to purchase the items. Wes won the argument about whether to buy a premade piecrust or make it homemade. Knowing he would end up with the hassle, Wes said *no way* to the homemade crust.

Putting the whole pie together only took Bray and Wes about fifteen minutes. They mixed sugar, cornstarch, salt, and cinnamon—then sprinkled it over the blueberries and poured the mixture into the piecrust that Luca had lined into the pan.

Bray cut the remaining pastry into thin strips and latticed the top, before Wes set the pie in the oven to bake.

"Do you mind if I go to Kyle's house for a little while? He's got this new video game for the Sega I want to play," Luca pleaded.

"You don't have to beg me to go to your friend's house. Go have fun for a while." Wes tilted his head in the direction of the front door.

Luca's friend Kyle lived down the street, and Luca still hadn't gotten over his excitement of living so close to him. He no longer had to bug Wes to drop him off and pick him up all the time.

"Okay, be back in a bit," Luca said and sprinted for the door.

Still feeling strange from the dream, Bray went outside to her tree and climbed up it. Peeking inside the tree hole, Bray let out a sigh because even though she knew he wouldn't be there, she wanted to look anyway. Brenik would have understood how she felt.

The heightened emotion had only come on this morning, and sometimes she had to let it run its course for a day or two to get back to herself.

"Are you trying to break your neck?" Wes shouted up to her.

Glancing down at the ground, she shook her head at him. "No, sometimes it feels good to climb and do things the hard way." She started to step down branch by branch, until she hopped down in front of him.

"You seem off today." He scanned her face, as if he could read her mind.

"Do I?" She was easy to read, because she wasn't very good at hiding her emotions.

"Yes, you know you do. Do you want to go inside and talk about it?" Wes asked, motioning his head at the back door.

"Can we talk out here?" Speaking about it outside in the open wouldn't be as constricting as being enclosed inside the house.

"We can talk anywhere you want to. Um, except for in your tree hole." He chuckled, gazing up at the open space—the window to her world.

Bray gave Wes's forearm a small poke. "Did you just make a joke?"

He rolled his eyes. "Maybe."

Squatting down on the grass, Bray propped her back up against the tree. Wes sat down beside her, straightening his legs all the way out before he leaned back.

"So, you know most of the story. But after our mother abandoned Brenik and me, one of the jovkins took care of us— kept us safe from others of her kind who wanted to slaughter our species. Junah wasn't overly affectionate, yet she was protective and made sure we had everything."

Even now, she still missed Junah, too.

"When we came here, we had Ruth. She was different, and I don't want to say better because they were both great in their own ways, but Ruth was caring and affectionate. And the thing is … I don't get to see her again or hear her voice. The day she had a heart attack, she asked us if we wanted peach pie, and we had said yes." A whimper escaped Bray's throat and she leaned her head forward, so she could reach up to brush away her tears. She brought her knees to her chest and hugged her legs.

An arm came down around her shoulder, and Wes pulled her close as she inhaled his woodsy cologne. He had never done anything like that before, but it was nice.

Wes propped the back of his head against the tree. "I'm not going to sit here and pretend I understand one word about the first half of what you said. And I don't think I want to know what a *jovkin* is. But you and Brenik didn't cause that heart attack—people die spontaneously all the time. I'm also not going to pretend like it still doesn't hurt me now because it sure as hell does sometimes, even though it's been almost six years." He let out a deep sigh, his throat bobbing. "For Luca, he's luckier in a sense because he doesn't remember our parents that well since he was still so young when they died. But I remember everything about them so clearly."

Bray removed her arms from her legs and looped one around Wes's waist. "Luca is incredibly lucky to have you."

"Thanks. That means a lot because I'm still learning as I go," Wes smiled warmly and looked down at her. "Seriously, if you ever need to talk about anything, don't hesitate. Okay?"

"Okay. But I never want to eat peach pie ever again." Bray wasn't sure why eating peaches didn't bother her, yet the thought of touching a peach pie was out of the question.

"No one's going to force you to eat peach pie, and I already told you that shit's nasty." He grimaced.

Bray buried her face into Wes's shoulder and let out a loud snort.

"Did you just get spit all over my shoulder?" He laughed while shrugging her off.

"Possibly?" She grinned, examining the wet spot on his shirt.

He looked down at his watch. "We should be getting back inside to check on our real pie that actually tastes good."

Thirteen

Brenik

Brenik observed himself in the mirror, noticing his tired eyes, just as a knock on the door signaled Rana was there to pick him up—at least he assumed it was her. After the night before with the police officer, he couldn't be sure.

Opening the door, Brenik found Rana's hesitant face. "Are you ready?" she asked shyly.

She looked different today, her hair grazed her neck with shorter layers framing her face. Unable to stop himself, Brenik reached out to touch a silky dark lock. "You cut your hair."

"I did. Hopefully, it doesn't look too bad. You show a hair stylist a picture, and it never turns out the same." She shrugged.

"I like it." And he did.

Her lips were reddened again by lipstick, and that small mole right below her lip had him wetting the center of his bottom lip with the tip of his tongue. He scanned the rest of her up and down, noticing the high waisted jeans with a short sleeve blouse that rested right above the waistband—showing a thin sliver of tawny skin.

"All right, let's go," she said. "There won't be too many of us tonight, but everyone should be there when we arrive."

"Let's roll," he said, trailing behind her.

Rana chatted during most of the drive—telling him about her teaching job at the local elementary school, and how she was hoping to save enough money to buy a house next year.

"You could always move in to my place," he suggested when she pulled into a parking space at her apartment building. Rana laughed hard at what she thought was a joke, but he wasn't joking. Then he remembered the owners would be back someday, so he would need to figure *that* out.

After walking up the flight of stairs to Rana's apartment, Brenik found six people seated around the cozy living room. Two women with short hair and one with braids sat on a blue fabric couch, two men with muscles at barstools, and one curly-haired guy sitting on the floor had a dimple in his chin.

"This is Brenik. Brenik, this is Jacob, Christopher, Adam, Kelly, Ashley, and my new roommate Josie." She pointed to each one individually, but by the time she got to the last person, he only remembered her roommate's—Josie's—name as they all waved.

Setting her purse down by the door, Rana turned to Brenik. "Do you want something to eat or drink? We have plenty of sodas, and I think Josie bought a ton of chips and dip."

Brenik ran a hand through his dark hair, already knowing he couldn't eat or drink anything. It hadn't seemed like it would be a big deal before, but not being able to eat or drink was becoming more tedious than he expected. Sooner or later Rana would start wondering why he always declined her offers. "Maybe later, I ate a big meal for dinner."

"No problem. You can take some home, too, because there will most likely be a ton left. Unless Adam eats everything." Rana tilted her head up toward one of the guys who had to be Adam. "Right, Adam?" Then she looked at Brenik, grinning widely.

Adam, with the brown curly hair, tapped his chest. "Who? Me? Now, why would I do such a thing?"

"You're holding the entire can of bean dip in your hand right now." Rana laughed and pointed to the dip several times.

"The power of bean dip." Adam lifted the can in the air and hugged it back at his chest, claiming his prize.

"You'll be remembering that later tonight when you're in the bathroom," one of the guys with muscles yelled. Brenik couldn't remember who he was.

Josie smacked the guy who yelled on the arm, and her braids swayed against her face. "You're disgusting, Jacob."

"It's true," Jacob responded, lifting a glass bottle to his mouth, trying not to smile.

Brenik watched on while everyone joked, and he quietly sat back and observed. If this was what normal felt like, then for the first time in his life, he had experienced it. The feeling was new and different, almost surreal.

"Who is this one again?" Brenik asked Rana as they went to sit on the floor next to one of the guys with long hair and muscles. He couldn't recall his name, but the guy's blond hair fell past his shoulders and he wore a blue and black flannel shirt.

"That's Christopher. He's a guitarist in a *band*, and they just switched over to grunge since that's 'what's in.'" She quoted in the air with her fingers as she rolled her eyes.

Christopher ticked his index finger back and forth at Rana. "I heard that, Rana. You'll see how great the band is when we have a live show."

Rana reached over and shook Christopher's arm. "You've been saying you're going to have a show for the past two years. When's it going to happen?"

"You can't rush perfection—and Greg's in need of a new muse." Christopher's attention turned to the extra curvy woman with short spiky hair, and he waggled his brows at her. "Kelly, are you up for the job?"

"That is a *no*. He's *fine* as hell, but he's been around the block a few too many times for me," Kelly answered.

Brenik found the whole conversation amusing.

Rana elbowed Brenik's bicep and leaned forward to speak close to his ear, her warm breath tickling the skin of his neck. "Greg's the singer in the band."

At that moment, Brenik wanted to take her any place where they could be alone. Even if it was just to talk.

"Time for charades," Josie yelled, and shook her arms at everyone.

The game was more interesting than Brenik thought it would be. He found himself not being overly communicative, but not completely anti-social either.

The group split up into four teams—the theme was Disney characters. Brenik hadn't bothered to watch most of the Disney movies—Bray would have known every answer.

Bobbing her arms stiffly up and down while bending her knees to lift her legs, Rana bulged her eyes and nodded toward Brenik.

"I don't have any idea what that even is." He chuckled as he tried to think about it.

"Wait, hang on," he added, holding up his hand over his eyes, so he could avoid being distracted by Rana's odd movements.

What is that movie Bray would watch with the girl who liked books? Brenik brought his other hand up, his fingers fiddling back and forth as he thought, while everyone in the room knew exactly who Rana was pretending to be. Then it came to him. "The Beast!" he shouted, content with his answer.

"What?" Rana yelled, throwing her hands up. "Are you kidding me? It's *Pinocchio*. You know? Puppet movements?" She dangled her arms again in his face with a cute, angry expression.

"Yeah, I have never seen that one." He shrugged a shoulder and grinned.

"I swear, you're from another planet." That was practically

true, and his grin grew wider as hers did the same, stretching across her face.

So beautiful.

After a few more rounds, everyone eventually left except for Rana and Brenik. Rana's roommate Josie went to stay the night at Jacob's house, who may or may not be her boyfriend. Rana said she could never tell.

She turned on a movie, and Brenik sat back against the couch, too distracted by her nearness to focus on the screen.

He placed his palm on the suede cushion, fingers pressing down into it. The barest touch of her skin met his.

It wasn't just the physical aspects of her he wanted—he yearned for all of her. But the all of her he craved wasn't agreeing with him, because that terrible hunger was trying to find its way out. If he didn't leave soon, Brenik feared the same thing would happen to her that had happened with Jeremy. Then all of her would become nothing, and he would not be okay with that.

"Rana, I have to leave," he rasped, already striding for the door.

"Oh, all right. Let me drive you home." Disappointment filled her voice, but he couldn't focus on that right now. Heat flooded his body, and his heart slammed against his chest, beating more rapidly than it ever had.

"Don't worry about it. It's right down the street—only a ten-minute walk," he stuttered.

"I'm taking you home," she said, her tone firm.

"I've got it. Thanks for having me over tonight." He tried to end the conversation as quickly as possible without it coming out too harsh.

"Sure." Her face fell.

His hands felt twitchy, but he didn't want to leave her like that. Before he left, he spun back around and said, "You know, your ex-boyfriend was a fucking idiot." Reaching out toward her lovely face, he brushed the pad of his thumb against her tiny mole.

"Do you want to come over tomorrow?" he asked.

"I'd love that. I can come a little after five." She smiled at him, the grim expression melting away. Brenik wanted to stay, but he had to hurry and leave.

"Good night, Rana." He dropped his hand from her face and turned around without looking back, for fear he would do something he'd regret.

Brenik's eyes flickered as he walked down the stairs, hands trembling against his jeans—Jeremy's jeans. He brushed away that thought. *Walk. Walk. Walk.* He had to tell himself to keep on walking. He needed to feed—*now*.

He knew. He *knew* what he would do this time and where he would go, because Jeremy was the wrong person to have stolen life from. Even though the aftermath had helped Brenik, Jeremy's face haunted him at night. Brenik was nothing but a stranger to him, and Jeremy had been kind enough to invite him into his home. And then look what happened.

Brenik shook the regret away.

Instead of turning right to head to his cabin, he took a left. Tall trees bordered the open area, and he lifted a branch out of the way, ducking under it. The city park was dim, and there were several people asleep up ahead—without anything or anyone.

An older man of around fifty with a graying beard sat at the edge of an iron bench. His head leaned all the way back, and soft gurgling snores escaped his wide-open mouth.

Reaching a finger out, Brenik tapped him softly on the shoulder. He didn't stir. The putrid combination of alcohol and filth reeking from the man's body filled his nostrils.

Scowling, Brenik shook the man's shoulder. The stranger's eyes fluttered opened as he stirred awake, his body flinching to the side when he saw Brenik hovering over him.

"Hey, man, I was seeing if you could help me with something," Brenik said.

The bearded man squinted one of his eyes, and his whole face contorted into a confused expression. "What do you need help with?" he asked and scratched the side of his balding head.

"I was in the forest earlier and somehow lost my car keys. If you help me search, I'll give you fifty bucks." Brenik patted his back pocket and tilted his head toward the wooded area.

"Even if we don't find them?" The man perked up.

"Yeah, but we need to hurry. I have work in the morning and don't want to be out here all night." Brenik's fingers twitched, and his heart slammed against his rib cage over and over. If the man didn't come with him soon, he was going to have to drain him right there on the spot.

Scanning the area, Brenik made sure the few other people around were still asleep, then he motioned the bearded man forward.

After walking for about a minute into the wooded area, Brenik couldn't take it anymore and whirled around. Before the man could yell, Brenik pushed a hand against the man's mouth and dove his protruding canines down into his victim's neck.

A soft chirping sound escaped the man's throat, his heavy breaths fading as Brenik drank. This wasn't like before—not the least bit lust filled—but the taste was ever blissful. Even with the grime of the man's neck pressing against Brenik's lips.

The smell of the dirt and the odor from the homeless man was making Brenik sick, but he couldn't stop because the blood was wondrous. The taste charged every nerve throughout his body and filled him with complete repletion.

When the last drop rested on his tongue, Brenik gently lay down the body. The blood lingered in his mouth, and he wanted to swallow, but he held it there.

Not many people ventured into those parts of the forest, but he dragged the body farther back anyway. He found a large bush and rolled the man underneath to cover him completely.

A hint of remorse ran through Brenik again, but he didn't know what else he could have done. It was either the old man who had nothing or Rana by accident. Brenik felt satisfied with the choice he had made.

He ran the remainder of the way to the cabin, hurrying to his bedroom. Before glancing up at the portrait, Brenik held his hand in front of his open mouth and let the blood drizzle into his palm.

Running his fingertip against the wet liquid, Brenik lifted his index finger and pushed it onto the painting.

The bright red fingerprint sat there for a moment, but then turned lighter and lighter before it vanished. Brenik shifted his eyes from the portrait to the mirror, watching as the tiredness of his eyes faded away and his face seemed to tighten back to its pristine beauty.

Attempting to smile at his reflection in the mirror, Brenik knew now how he would be able to live a life and get what he wanted. Even though it would eat at him.

Fourteen

Bray

"**Y**ou're home early," Bray said to Wes as he walked through the living room door.

"I'm on my way to pick up Luca, and I wanted to see if you'd come eat with us at the park. If you want to?" Wes asked.

Bray loved going to the park. Most of the time she would sit in the trees and watch families spending time together or people walking their dogs. The day and nightlife of the park were literally like night and day. After dark, the people who had no homes would gather and seek companionship.

Clapping her hands together, she smiled brightly. "What are we going to eat?"

Wes rolled his eyes. "Luca wants McDonald's. I can't stomach it ninety percent of the time, but we take turns picking where to eat. Maybe I should tell him it's your turn."

She thought about it for a moment. "I'll choose McDonald's. They have great fries."

Wes shook his head and gave a false huff. "Overly salted fries, but McDonald's it is. You know, this two against one thing is getting out of hand already."

"Would bringing the remaining pie cheer you up?" There

was still half of the blueberry pie from yesterday left. It had tasted magical.

"You're back on my good side for reminding me about that." Wes grabbed the pie from the kitchen, while Bray watched his back muscles flex under his tight white shirt. It was hard for her to not stare at him when he wasn't looking.

Before Wes and Bray could pick up Luca, they had to wait in the car line for a long time first. Bray chatted away to Wes, who mainly listened instead of doing any talking.

"What would you rather have happen: parachute not open as you fall from the sky or boat sink in the middle of an ocean with no life jacket?" she asked, propping her chin in between her thumb and index finger, tilting her head at him.

Wes's brow furrowed. "What the hell kind of question is that?"

"It's a what if question."

"To answer your morbid question, since I'm scared of heights, it would have to be the ocean one."

She thought about it for a second before giving a reply. "That's hypocritical, though."

Shaking his head and tossing up his arms, he laughed. "How is *that* hypocritical?"

"The ocean itself is thousands of feet deep. So you being in the middle of the sea is the same as being high up off the ground."

His eyes widened as he straightened in his seat. "What? That's the dumbest thing I've ever heard. There's still water between you and the ocean floor, so I wouldn't be falling to my death."

"You're right. You would slowly be sinking to your death with unknown creatures just below your feet." Bray held up her hands and creepily wiggled her fingers in his face.

Wes grabbed her hand and pulled her closer to him, causing a gasp to escape her mouth. "Would they grab me like this?" He smiled, biting his lip.

They stared at each other for a moment, Wes's gaze falling from her eyes to her mouth and right back up.

The door to the backseat opened, and Wes dropped her hand as Luca entered the car. Bray cleared her throat and leaned back. "Yes, that's exactly what they would do."

"Hey, guys." Luca beamed and buckled himself up.

Bray craned her neck around the seat to peer at Luca as she reached for the door handle. "Do you want to sit up front?"

"No way, you can have shotgun." Then he tapped Wes on the shoulder. "McDonald's?"

"McDonald's," Wes replied, and shot Luca a disgusted face with his tongue sticking out.

When they arrived at the park, Luca grabbed the bag of food, Wes got the drinks, and Bray carried the pie. The steaming food had smelled so good in the car.

There was already a crowd of people at the park. Two appeared to be flying kites since the wind was blowing the right speed. They waved back and forth in the sky. As Bray found herself studying the diamond shapes, her head seemed to be swaying from side to side along with them.

Wes glanced at her and then at the sky, raising a brow. "You going to kite dance all day?"

"Maybe." She found it rather calming.

"Okay, I'll watch right along with you, but let's eat first." He looked at the McDonald's bag in Luca's hand and crinkled his nose. "Or maybe not." Luca was already digging in and stuffing a handful of fries in his mouth, rubbing the salt and grease on the side of his shorts.

Bray fished her hand inside the bag and grabbed a fry, plopping it into her mouth as she took a seat under a large oak tree beside Wes and Luca. The thick branches were outstretched and provided the right amount of shade.

Wes pulled out his Big Mac and ate it like he had never eaten before.

"I thought you didn't like McDonald's?" Bray challenged.

"I don't, but I'm ravenous." He took another huge bite of the burger.

"He *says* he doesn't like McDonald's," Luca piped in, "but between you and me, Bray, I know he loves it."

"You got me, Lu. I wanted to keep the truth away, but I'll admit the sauce in the Big Mac gets me every time," Wes confessed with a mouthful of hamburger.

Bray finished her chicken nuggets and set the box aside. With the plastic utensils in the McDonald's bag, she used the knife to cut them each a slice of pie.

After she had her first taste of it yesterday, she decided blueberry pie was her new favorite. And today, she realized as she swallowed the last bite, it was still going to stay that way.

Luca reached for the paper bag and stuffed his trash inside. "Wes, I'm going to swing for a while. Is that okay?"

"Sure, Lu. We'll be walking around if you need us." Wes pointed at the surrounding track.

Luca walked off to sit beside a blonde girl, and he immediately started chatting with her. So, *that* was why he wanted to go swing. Bray smiled at the cute scene, watching as he kept brushing his bangs away from one of his brows.

When they had finished eating, Bray and Wes threw away their trash except for the drinks, before they walked the dirt track. She looked up and the two kites from earlier weren't flying anymore, but a new one was in their place—a red Chinese dragon.

Turning to Wes, Bray studied him for a second. "Were you like Luca when you were younger?"

Wes stretched his neck out to glance at Luca on the swings. "With the ladies?"

She giggled and swatted his arm.

Wes chuckled softly. "Luca's a lot more outgoing than I was. In fact, I was sort of nerdy throughout elementary and junior high."

"What changed?" She couldn't imagine Wes ever being

nerdy.

"I grew taller, better hair—that's about it." He dramatically brushed a lock of hair behind his ear and smiled.

The top of Bray's head reached his shoulder, so she supposed he was tall. She wondered why he didn't have a woman in his life now. At first when she met him, she could understand why—he had been grumpy that first night. But now he wasn't so bad.

"So, why don't you have a girlfriend?"

"Hmm?" he asked as he took a sip of his soda, smiling as he drank.

"Shut up, you heard me."

Still smiling, he pulled the drink away from his mouth. "You don't want to hear about my non-existent romantic life."

"I do." She really did.

"Well … in high school I dated around, but my first year of college I had a serious girlfriend. Once my grandpa passed away, though, I didn't have time for it—or for her—from trying to get everything settled with Luca. She didn't quite understand that." He shrugged.

"What a jerk." Bray didn't understand who wouldn't want to be around Luca.

"In her defense, when we started dating I didn't have a kid, but then suddenly I did, and we were both only nineteen." Bray still didn't understand. She was twenty now, which wasn't much older, and didn't find it a big deal.

"You haven't been with anyone since then?"

Wes's face flushed, and he looked down when he answered. "So, there have been times when Luca has stayed the night somewhere … when I've seen some women, but nothing over the past six months." That didn't seem too long ago to Bray.

"Mine was a year ago after Ruth passed away," she rushed out. "Only I've never had a boyfriend, just that one time."

Wes's eyes widened in complete surprise. "You mean you—"

Something shoved Bray from behind before he could finish his sentence, her drink dropping from her hand as she hit the ground. Tight fists pounded at her back, and she screamed from the sharp pain. As she tried to flip to her back, the weight was lifted off of her.

Chest heaving, Bray rolled over and stood to see Wes restrain a man, securing his arms behind his back. The man had a gray beard and wore dirty ragged clothing. His lips were pulled back into a sneer, and he was growling.

"Bray, go get the security guard at the front," Wes grunted out, barely able to contain the man. He was straining against Wes, shaking and eyeing her with rage. Behind his back, the man's fingers flexed and twitched, inhumanly.

The crazed man's head twisted over his shoulder to Wes. Dried blood rested around two puncture wounds on his filthy neck—similar to the other man, named Jeremy Jones, who had been shot in their neighborhood.

Before Bray could dart off to the front, the man bucked and writhed frantically, causing Wes to lose his grip. The man took off, growling. Wes had already started to run after him, but Bray wasn't going to let Wes go after the lunatic alone.

"Stay back," Wes yelled at her.

Bray was fast, faster than Wes. She picked up her speed and surged forward, pushing them both to the ground. The insane man jerked roughly, and Bray couldn't hold him down. He leaped up, knocking her to the dirt, and took off again.

"What the hell? Are you okay?" Wes panted as he helped her off the ground. "What just happened?"

She had no clue, but adrenaline continued to flow through her veins. "I'm okay, let's hurry and find Luca." Bray scanned the area until she focused on his small frame.

As they approached Luca, he was still chatting away with the blonde girl on the swing. "Luca, we have to go now," Wes called, motioning for him to hurry up.

"Already?" Luca asked, disappointment written all over his

face.

"*Now*, Luca!"

Luca gave a solemn sigh and said something to the girl before coming up to them. "What's going on, Wes? We don't—"

"Not now. Bray's hurt," Wes said hurriedly.

Bray waved him off. "I'm fine."

Wes looked past Bray and sped off. Turning around, she spotted the security guard. Wes was already ranting and pointing in the direction that the deranged man had gone off in.

Walking back toward them, Wes looked pissed. "I don't even know why some of these people have jobs if they don't want to do the damn work. The security guard said he was going to search around and write up a report. He didn't appear too worried about it, and he said he hadn't seen the guy." Wes turned to her. "Seriously, Bray, are you okay?"

"I told you I'm fine, Wes. Also, the guy isn't a real security guard. They just volunteer during the day hours."

Ignoring the part about the security guard, Wes lifted the back of her shirt up a little to examine her skin. "Your back's red, and it may bruise." Her back did feel sore but not too bad.

"I'll be okay. I think we should go home, though."

The edges of Luca's lips turned downward, but she didn't want anything to happen to him.

Back at the house, Luca pulled out his homework from his huge backpack and set the paper down on the coffee table to work on it.

Wes turned on the TV, still scowling about the entire incident.

"Another man has been shot and killed as he tried to attack

two teenagers walking home from basketball practice. One suffered a broken arm, and the other numerous scratch marks. A policeman who drove by saw the incident and intervened. Details from the crime scene revealed there was no blood from the shot wound of the attacker. There were also two punctured holes found on the side of his neck. We are still waiting to find out the identity of the unknown man and are unsure if this case is connected to the one we previously reported. We will keep you informed," the female reporter stated.

Wes's wide eyes fixed on Bray. "That's the same guy. You saw the two punctured holes on the side of his neck."

Bray nodded because she most certainly did. The two incidents had to be connected. She didn't have a clue how and wasn't sure if she really wanted to know.

Fifteen

Brenik

Rana knocked on Brenik's door a little after five. He was still full and satisfied from feeding on the homeless man the night before.

He opened the door to see her wearing jeans, a floral print shirt, and a smile on her face. "Come on in."

"I have a better idea," she announced. "Let's go out to eat—I'm craving Mexican food."

Brenik's stomach shuddered at the thought of eating, but he still tried to hide his revulsion and appear thrilled.

She must have noticed his slight grimace, though. "What, you don't like enchiladas smothered in sauce?"

He couldn't say he did. "No, but I can see what else they offer."

"I don't know if I can be your friend anymore," she joked.

Brenik felt fine earlier, but now he was suffocating again. The food situation was going to destroy him, and he didn't know what the fuck he was going to do about eating at that place. He sure as hell couldn't just sit there and watch her chow down.

"Is that what we are, *friends*?" he teased, brushing away his anxiety.

She stayed quiet after his response. He knew she wanted him as much as he did her, even if she pretended not to.

After hopping in Rana's car and her driving for about fifteen minutes, she pulled into a narrow parking lot. The restaurant was once a house, and a crooked sign out front read: *Maria's Mexican Food.* Brenik wasn't impressed.

"Don't get that stupid look on your face. This place has the best Mexican food you will ever have in your entire life."

Brenik glanced up at the peeling pink paint and the patchy roof shingles. "I'm sure it does," he replied sarcastically.

"It does!" She thrust her index finger at the building.

Brenik held both hands up. "Okay, okay, I believe you."

The restaurant appeared larger on the inside than the outside. There were four small square tables, and wooden chairs with padded green cushions pushed into each spot.

They seated themselves at one of the tables near the front door. A short woman with a copper complexion, and streaks of gray throughout her black hair, set down two paper menus in front of them, followed by a basket of chips and red salsa. When the waitress asked for their drink orders, Brenik just mumbled, "Water."

The basket lingered in front of him. He didn't find chips pleasurable, even when he could eat normal food. It was a good thing he didn't have to pretend not to like their throat-cutting, knife-like edges.

"What? You don't like chips either?" Rana asked, smiling as she grabbed a chip.

"No. They scratch my throat to the point where it feels like it may bleed," Brenik said, his voice serious.

"Overdramatic, are we?"

"No, I just know what I like." He held her stare, his heart beating faster, his body heating. She was the first to look away, her eyes tilting down at the menu.

Brenik pulled up the yellow paper in front of his face and scanned over the items. He thought he could try to sound out the words, but he was unable to read them. Maybe he could ask for some type of animal blood to test out. *No, Rana would probably be too weirded out about that idea.* He knew they had to have quesadillas, so he would try that.

The waitress came back and set their drinks in front of them. Rana went ahead and ordered the three-cheese enchilada plate. The sound of it was making his stomach heave just thinking about it.

"I'll take a chicken quesadilla," he said, holding back the bile. The smiling waitress wrote down their order and walked away.

"You'll love it, I swear," Rana promised and placed her hand against her chest. He almost believed her—*almost.*

When the plates came, he studied the quesadilla like it was an enemy he was trying to turn into a companion. He ate one slice and although it tasted like paper—which he knew because he had tried to eat paper before—it stayed down.

Patting his stomach and smiling broadly, he gave his abdomen one more rub to fake the delight. Rana's eyebrows were battling which direction to go as she watched him—one stayed up, and the other one hunched down.

But Brenik knew it. He fucking knew it. And he should have stopped there. As soon as he swallowed the first bite of the second slice, Brenik gagged and uncontrollably heaved.

Rana's brows figured out what to do at that moment as they both flew up in distress. "Are you okay?" She shot up and skirted the table, slamming her hand against his back. "Do you need me to do the Heimlich?

No, he didn't need her to perform the fucking Heimlich so he could shoot black shit all over the table. Throwing down the cloth napkin, Brenik took off in the direction leading to the bathroom, a thick sludge slowly crawling up his throat.

The bathroom smelled like piss because some jackass didn't know how to aim his dick at a toilet. Avoiding the splashes of urine on the floor, Brenik hurled and a long, black worm-shaped thing came up and dropped into the water, splashing him in the process.

Brenik didn't care—he just wanted the shit up and for this to stop. Grabbing his hair and moping over to the small rectangular mirror, he pulled the locks so hard that some strands were left in between his fingers when he let go.

Enough. He'd had *enough.* No more food of any kind unless it was human blood—someone worthless.

Glaring at whatever was in his way, Brenik scuffed his feet out of the bathroom to a worried Rana. She gnawed at the edge of her lip and blinked one too many times.

"That was *not* the best food I've had in my entire life," he said as horror crossed her face. But he couldn't help but smirk at her reaction.

Rana pulled something out of her purse. "Gum?" she asked and handed him a stick.

Despite not wanting another thing in his mouth right then, Brenik reached for the silver wrapper, unfolded it, and stuck the gum in his mouth. "Thanks." As long as he didn't swallow it, he would be more than fine.

Rana apologized several times on the way back to his house. It wasn't her fault, and he told her that. She assured him he could choose a place the next time they went out to eat.

Brenik just nodded and smiled, attempting to seem enthused. When he turned his head to gaze out the window, he shut his eyes for a moment, trying to clear his head. Too many dark thoughts swirled in there, and he didn't want any of them.

"Do you want to come inside?" Brenik asked when he reached for the door handle after Rana parked the car.

"I would, but I have to finish grading a whole stack of papers I neglected over the weekend."

Disappointment hit Brenik, but he understood. "Maybe another day?"

"How about Friday? I can leave work straight away if you want to catch a movie."

A movie sounded nice. It would be another way to feel normal.

"I can meet you at your work," he said. "The school is close by here, anyway."

"If you really feel like walking." She grinned. He didn't mind it one bit, especially if it was to see her.

Opening the door to step out of the car, Brenik instead pulled back and closed it. He leaned toward Rana, and fiercely pushed his mouth against hers. There was no way he was going to leave this car without a kiss from those red lips that he had been craving to touch, taste.

Rana stilled and Brenik wasn't going to force her lips to move, but a moment later, she caressed his with hers, gentle, inviting, then deepening. Her lips searched and explored before her tongue entered his mouth, meeting his, driving him wild.

Brenik reached down and pushed the button to unlock her seat belt. She was too far away. His hand lightly entwined in her hair as the other pressed on her back to draw her closer. As he leaned back, she came with him, keeping her mouth on his while she crawled on top of him.

He wanted her. He wanted her so damn bad as her lips left his and trailed down his neck. Brenik's skin was filled with triggers and nerve endings on edge. Pushing her waist down, he ground his hips against her, feeling her, wanting her, needing her to get closer.

But Brenik knew she had to leave and he reluctantly moved her face away. Then he drew her back to kiss her slowly once more, and not so needy this time. Even though he craved more, it felt good nonetheless.

Rana moved back and rested her forehead on his. "So, Friday?"

"Friday," he whispered as he angled down to the crook of her neck to kiss her there for a moment. No urge or desire to feed off her plagued him.

With swollen lips, Rana settled back in her seat, appearing shy as her cheeks flushed.

"I knew you could be an animal if you wanted to," he purred, not able to take his gaze off her.

"Whatever, just leave." She laughed and rolled her eyes at him, but he could see yearning there, too.

Brenik headed inside the cabin, where he would need to take care of himself on his bed.

Brenik would be seeing Rana in a couple days, and he had an idea he wanted to try. It was something he should have attempted earlier, and he needed to find an animal. There were plenty of those around the forested area of his cabin.

He remembered the raccoons living underneath the house, and he debated crawling beneath the cabin. But those creatures were intelligent, and it smelled of feces down there, so he tossed that idea away.

The damn squirrel was too fast as he dodged for it, and the furry animal darted straight up the tall tree. Another idea stirred in Brenik's mind as he watched the squirrel scurry past a bird's nest. The tiny chirping struck his ears, and he let out a small sigh for what he was about to do. Why he felt worse about killing a baby bird over a human being, he wasn't sure. Maybe because humans had choices. The homeless man didn't have to be a drunk. Jeremy, on the other hand, was a regret that continued to fester inside his head.

Swallowing his dread, Brenik effortlessly climbed up the thin pine branches that somehow managed to hold his weight. When he reached the next limb, he quietly peered over the edge of the nest and saw two small baby sparrows. He didn't know whether to separate them or take them both, but he decided to leave one for the mother bird.

Tenderly, he lifted the little sparrow as it squeaked and writhed its tiny head, smacking its beak open and closed.

Climbing back down was more of a struggle with the bird in his hand. He didn't want to perform the deed outdoors, so he walked the little bird inside the cabin, stroking its gray and pink back each step of the way.

When Brenik reached the kitchen, the creature ceased making any noise as it looked up with something... Trust? It wasn't trust he was trying to provide, but a comfort for what he was about to do.

Closing his eyes, Brenik swiftly twisted the bird's fragile neck to the right, and a light crack echoed through the cabin. Brenik opened his eyes and looked down at the lost life—he hated being a predator.

Brenik pulled open the kitchen drawer and drew out a knife. Lowering the blade to the sparrow's stomach, he cut a small line and watched blood bloom to the surface. Then he brought the fragile body to his lips and drank, the taste of metal filling his mouth. A satisfaction instantly hit him—it worked. Not that he wanted to kill baby birds forever, but if that was what he had to do, then he would do it.

Resting the dead sparrow on the counter, Brenik went into his room and pressed the last drop of blood to the portrait. The canvas absorbed it, but no sensations stirred within him.

Something was off, but he ignored the feeling and picked up the bird to go bury it outside. After he finished covering the small creature with dirt, he felt it, his abdomen twisting, tightening. The urge to get the heinous thing out of his stomach.

Brenik would not do it. He was going to hold it down because he had found a new way of fulfilling the task. The unsettling truth was that he hadn't.

He dug the palm of his hand into the bark of the tree, firmly keeping his lips sealed. But it came back up in a thick black solid form like all the other times. Brenik squeezed the bark as hard as he could, staring down at his blackened failure.

Defeated, he yanked his hand away from the tree and gazed at the hairline scratches left behind on his palm. Brenik needed help, and he needed to talk to Bray.

When the day grew dark, Brenik headed back to the tree hole. A red truck and a blue car sat lifelessly in the cracked driveway—the house seemed to be fully moved into already.

A sinking emotion enveloped him—it was as if Ruth had never been there at all. The porch was lit, spilling its glow across freshly-planted blue and white flowers in the front yard.

Lights were on in the house, and Brenik thought maybe he should have waited until an even later time. He quietly rounded the corner of the house and opened the gate—a small amount at a time to avoid any squeaking.

The back porch was lit, too, and he silently cursed to himself, but at least he was able to see well. A light illuminated in Ruth's old sewing room, and he couldn't help peering in through a small gap in the curtains.

A young boy with dark hair was in the room, lying on his stomach in bed while reading a thick book.

Brenik backed away from the scene inside the room and headed for the tree. He stayed as silent as possible and easily found his way up the trunk to the hole.

"Psst… Bray, it's me," he spoke softly. No response. She may already be asleep, but he couldn't see inside. "Bray," he said again.

When she didn't answer, Brenik snaked his hand inside to wake his sister on her hammock. It was empty, so he moved his fingertips to his bed. Nothing except for the cloth. She wasn't there.

Well, where the hell is she? Brenik shrugged off his

disappointment, because he couldn't expect her to sit around all day long in a tree hole, waiting for him to return. But he was used to it—she had always been there when he came back.

He would try another day, or maybe he wouldn't. Another idea came to him.

It had been a while since he had drunk human blood. The urge would be coming soon. He didn't want to be near Rana when it happened, so he would have to hunt before that.

Climbing down the tree, Brenik hurried out of the backyard and closed the gate without making a single peep.

Quickening his pace down the street, he headed straight for the park. Brenik didn't know what would happen once he finished off the homeless strays in that area. Eventually, he would have to find some elsewhere.

Security was gone for the night, and there lay several people inside the park already sleeping—some were still up doing suspicious-looking activities.

When he had murdered the homeless man—whose real name he found out was Larry Thibodeaux—he thought the people staying at the park would be too scared to come back. Lucky for Brenik, when Larry somehow came back to life, he had left the park premises.

Maybe he didn't actually murder them when he drank their blood, which made him feel a little better about killing them.

From what the news had said, the attackers were crazy with rage. He found it odd that they didn't change into what he was and pine for blood instead.

Brushing off his thoughts, Brenik stalked toward a woman in her late forties with stringy russet hair. A stretchy band was tied around her arm as she slid a needle into a vein at her inner elbow. *What a waste of a human.* But he was there to end her suffering.

Brenik knelt beside her and purred in her ear, "Hey, Darlin', how are you this evening?"

She looked up at him with a glare, but didn't hide the needle that was still in her closed fist. "Screw off."

Feisty. "Do you want to go somewhere?" Brenik felt his pulse quicken, not really wanting to do it, but he had to fight the remorse that would come later.

"I won't go anywhere with you, pretty boy. Unless you want to pay me," the woman said with an inkling of seduction, as she pulled her shoulders back to puff out her sunken chest and breasts.

"How about we go into the bushes, and I'll pay you a hundred bucks?"

Grinning with a mouthful of blackened and cracked off teeth, she said, "I would have done it for ten."

Furrowing his brow, Brenik helped the woman up—her hand was filthy and the skin dry. Pity struck him for a moment that this woman was willing to give herself to some strange person for only ten dollars. With the gift he was about to give her, she wouldn't have to deal with those situations anymore.

They walked to the same place where Brenik had brought Larry. The woman stumbled, and Brenik grabbed her arm to keep her from falling. "What's your name?" he asked.

"Claire," she slurred with flirtation.

He grimaced at her teeth as she smiled at him. "Claire, why do you do this?"

"For money, you idiot." Maybe he wasn't feeling guilty anymore.

"Do you like living?"

"Not at the moment, no." Claire didn't even look sad when she shook her head.

"Okay, let me help you." Ignoring the stench of her unbathed skin, Brenik drew her more than willing body close to him.

Dodging her mouth as she leaned in to kiss him, Brenik rested his forehead against her shoulder and let his canines slide down. Without waiting any longer, since her hand was creeping near his crotch, he sank his teeth into her throat.

Claire gasped in pleasure—he knew it was partly from her high and partly from him. The flavor was immaculate and highlighted all that was good as it traveled down to the organ lusting for it.

The last bit of blood remained in his mouth when he lay the woman on the ground. Chest heaving, he gently closed her wide-open eyes.

She didn't have to suffer anymore.

Brenik took off in a rush to get back home to the painting. Throwing open the door, he hurried inside while the blood stayed in his mouth and mixed with his saliva.

Above the dresser, the painting, as usual, seemed to be studying him. Avoiding its gaze, he spat the blood into the palm of his hand and pressed the red liquid onto the picture. He watched as the portrait drank it away.

A shift in him happened immediately, and he felt as if he was being sewn back together with pieces he didn't know were already separating—everything tightening back into place.

Running his clean fingertip against the outline of his face in the painting, Brenik then turned to the mirror. He moved his eyes back and forth, his infatuation with the image of himself growing.

Brenik had to turn away from the reflection as he became more and more hypnotized. There was now a way that made it possible for him to feed and not feel completely haunted. Collapsing onto the floor, he pushed his back up to the dresser and closed his eyes. At that moment, Brenik knew he was losing parts of himself.

Sixteen

Bray

Over the past week, Bray had spent most of her time writing in one of Wes's spare spiral notebooks. When the boys were at work and school, she would read but found she enjoyed writing, too.

She had started working on a story for kids around Luca's age with fantastical creatures that existed in Laith. Not that anyone would have to know about that, except for the three of them—and Brenik.

Brenik still hadn't returned, and she was beginning to get worried. *What if he never came back?*

The doorknob turned while Bray was in the middle of her reverie, and she thought for a moment that it was Brenik. But it was only Luca.

She gave him a warm smile. "Hey, Luca. How was your day?"

Tossing his backpack beside the doorframe, Luca shut the door. "It was awesome. Miss Alvi said the whole class did such an excellent job on their tests, that we got to have a movie and popcorn party at the end of the day."

"Cool! What movie did you watch?" Bray asked as she folded one of the pages over in her notebook.

"*FernGully*." He smiled deviously.

She blinked. "Don't even say it."

"Crysta definitely looks like you if you were to cut your hair off."

"Too bad her wings are clear and a completely different shape." They looked nothing like Bray's.

"Still, a very close resemblance." Luca laughed as he headed for the fridge and poured himself a glass of milk—drinking it in only a few gulps.

Bray closed her spiral notebook and set her pen on top. She would work on her story tomorrow. Tossing her braid over her shoulder, she met Luca in the kitchen.

"What time are you going to your friend's house?" she asked.

Luca was already on his second cup of milk, finishing it up. "Right now. You want to walk with me?"

"Okay."

The night before, Luca had begged Wes to let him stay the night at Kyle's house. Wes said *no way* at first, since it was a school night. But Kyle's mom guaranteed the boys would be in bed by nine and she'd take them to school in the morning. He ended up giving in to Luca and telling him just this one time.

"Let me go get my bag for the night," Luca said, starting for his room.

"Wes wanted me to make sure you finished your homework before you left. Do you have any?" Bray yelled down the hall.

Luca rounded the corner with his overstuffed bag. Bray wasn't sure what he had in there since he was only going to be staying at Kyle's for one night, but she let him do as he pleased.

"I didn't have any today since I finished all my math questions in class." Luca snapped both of his fingers, extra proud of himself.

"Great. Let's go."

When they stepped outside, a slight breeze ruffled Luca's hair. Kyle's house was only seven down from theirs, so it wouldn't take long to walk him.

"What are you going to do with me gone for the night?" Luca asked.

"Probably watch one of your movies." There were still a lot of them she hadn't seen.

"*FernGully*?" He waggled his brows.

Bray tapped the tip of his freckled nose. "No, not that one. I want to watch a movie I haven't seen."

"Maybe a scary one, so you can tell Wes to hold you tight." Luca wrapped his arms around himself in a pretend hug.

Bray threw her head back and laughed. "Whatever, I can hold my own self tight. *And* I don't get scared during movies."

He shut one eye and stared up at the bright blue sky, scrunching up his face. "I'll think of a good one to watch this weekend, and I'll bet you a hundred bucks it'll scare you."

"I don't have any money, and I'm sure you don't have a hundred bucks either."

Luca rubbed at his chin for a moment. "Chores. If I win, you can do my chores."

"And if I win, you can read me a *really* long story." She would be reading her own story to herself while he was gone.

"Deal." He stuck out his hand, and she shook it.

They stepped onto the beginning of Kyle's driveway. "Have a good night, little beast."

"See you tomorrow, Bray." Smiling, Luca turned and headed for his friend's door.

Bray waited until a boy with red hair, who must have been Kyle, answered. Waving goodbye to them, Bray walked back home and headed through the gate to her tree. She climbed the branches to check inside in case Brenik may have popped up. Her stomach sank when she realized nothing had changed—he wasn't home.

Plucking a plump peach, she climbed back down the

branches and brought the fruit to her mouth. Just as she swallowed her first bite, she heard the engine of Wes's work truck pull into the driveway.

She ducked down behind the gate, chewing more of the peach as she waited for Wes to approach. The pounding of his shoes tapped against the pavement as his steps drew closer.

"Surprise!" she yelled and leaped from behind the gate, throwing her arms up while waving them side to side.

"Jesus Christ, Bray. Seriously," Wes hissed, taking a step back with a hand covering his forehead.

"I promise I won't do it anymore." She smiled and put her palm against her chest, where her heart was buried beneath.

Wes stared at her hand, looking unimpressed. "Are you trying to do the Pledge of Allegiance? Besides, you told me that yesterday." Indeed, she had said that when she sprung out at him in the hallway the night before.

"I'm serious this time." She meant it at that moment, but her mind could change.

"Uh huh. I'll believe it when I see it." He smiled and strode for the front door.

Closing the gate, Bray followed behind him. "Luca already went over to Kyle's house. He had already finished all his homework at school."

"Good. Thanks for checking with him on that. Hopefully, they actually go to bed when Kyle's mom tells them to. But I have a feeling they'll try to stay up late. It's something I would do."

She was pretty sure Luca and Kyle would probably try to play video games with the sound of the TV on mute.

"I don't mind at all. It's the least I could do for you after allowing me to stay in the house," Bray said.

His expression softened as he opened the door, obviously grateful. "You've really helped me out. You keep the house clean, even though I don't ask you to. So, now I don't have to hire a maid. Really, it's like I'm saving money." He crinkled his nose and looked a little scared for a moment. "You know you don't have to do that stuff, right?"

Bray liked doing it, though. Especially when she could blast the music from Wes's stereo. "I know, but I want to." She smiled.

"Let me hurry and take a shower before I contaminate any of your freshly cleaned floors." He grinned.

Bray reached for her notebook and plotted some more ideas out. She was in the middle of making a list of character names, when she heard the shower turn on and the clank of feet entering the ceramic tub.

Something about being in the house while Wes was showering felt different than usual. He didn't have any clothes on. *Of course he doesn't have clothes on. He's in the shower!*

Usually when Wes got home and bathed, Luca was already there, or she was outside and not focused on what he was doing. This was Wes she was thinking about. Yes, he was beautiful. She had been aware of his good looks since the first time she spotted him from the tree. *I have to stop.*

Going outside to get some fresh air helped clear her head. There was a splash that swished in the direction of the birdbath. A blackbird was happily flapping its feathered wings in the clear water—she had changed it out earlier.

After trying to distract herself for what had to have been enough time, Bray went back inside, finding Wes in the kitchen preparing a frozen pizza.

He wore his usual fitted black T-shirt and a pair of cargo shorts, his wet hair curling on the ends.

Wes glanced at her as he set the pepperoni pizza on a pan. "Hungry?"

She stared at the pizza with longing. "I'm famished."

"Can you survive twenty-five minutes?" he asked.

"Maybe? How will you keep me entertained?"

"Possibly music or a movie," Wes answered, placing the pizza in the oven and starting the timer.

Bray went into the living room and pulled out Wes's huge CD case from the shelf beside the TV. She had listened to a lot of the albums while he was gone, but she hadn't made it through everything.

So far, the Cure and the Smashing Pumpkins were her two favorites. Ruth had mostly listened to the oldies, so Bray had to catch up on music from the past couple of decades.

Wes perched down beside her on the floor and watched her flip through the plastic pages. He shot a hand forward and plucked out a disc from the sleeve.

"Have you listened to this one yet?" he asked, balancing the perfectly round disc with his index finger through the hole in the middle.

Peering down at the CD, Bray read the words: *The Cranberries.* "No, but it sounds delicious."

"Oh, it is." He grinned and popped the CD into the big stereo beside the TV, pressing play.

Bray lay back on the carpeted floor as the first song played—a slow yet powerful melody that pulled at each and every one of her nerve fibers. Wes lowered himself beside her, his arm brushing hers.

Her eyes were closed, and she didn't look at him as she absorbed each beat, each note, each breath from the female voice—it was *breathtaking.*

She almost forgot where she was for a moment. The only thing that kept her grounded was Wes's arm still firmly pressed against hers. Opening her eyes, she turned her head to look at him. He was watching her with something new burning in his gaze: part intense, part sweet.

The next song started, and she *knew* it—not the name of it—but she had heard it in a movie somewhere.

Before Wes could react, Bray was on her feet and reached her hand out for his. "Dance with me?" she asked him, bouncing in place.

"You want me to dance?" He laughed and arched a brow at

her like she was insane.

"Yes!" She wiggled her fingers in front of him. He closed his eyes and shook his head but grabbed her hand anyway, fighting a smile.

She was terrible, he was terrible—but they were terrible together. His entire body was too stiff as he nodded and shuffled his feet side to side. She was overly energetic as she hopped around in circle after circle, not growing the least bit exhausted.

Once the song came to an end, Wes went to sit back down, and she stopped him. "Just one more. Please?"

"Since you said please and all, okay. But let me pick the song."

"Okay!" she said eagerly.

Wes pressed the next button on the stereo several times and stood back in front of her. "The last song already tired me out, so I picked a slower one this time," he said as the next track started to play. "I'm only twenty-three and feel so old." He chuckled.

Wes held his hand out to Bray, and she placed hers in his. They talked and swayed, and he attempted to spin her in a circle. That didn't work out too well, but it made them laugh. Then he pulled her closer to his body—the closeness doing something to her insides—something jittery, warming.

Bray's eyes were drawn to his mouth, then up to that small pale scar on the side of his upper lip. Her gaze finally met his as he stared down at her. They studied each other for what felt like hours when in reality the moment only lasted a few minutes.

Without thinking, she looked back at his scar and reached her hand up, brushing her finger delicately against the skin. His eyes closed at her touch, and she asked, "How did you get that?"

He snapped his head forward, and she yelped out of surprised as he softly bit her finger.

"Got ya. You're hard to scare," he whispered, and she playfully narrowed her eyes at him. "There isn't a battle wound story for me to tell you. I got it when I was learning to ride my bike. When I fell on the grass, a sharp piece of glass cut me. My mom freaked out, but it wasn't bad enough to need stitches or anything."

"You're right, that was a lousy story," she said mockingly.

"Was it?" he challenged, pulling her closer.

"It was." There was no real force in her words as her face drifted up to his.

"What a shame," he drawled. Then his mouth was on hers, just as the oven timer went off, letting them know the pizza was ready.

Seventeen

Bray

The pizza is ready. Startled, Bray left her mouth glued to Wes's, even with the annoying buzz of the alarm going off.

Wes lifted his face from hers, a gleam in his eyes as he gazed at her. "Screw that pizza," he said, and his mouth collided with hers once more. His mouth caressed hers, lips moving in sync, then he stepped back too soon. "Okay, wait right here. Don't go anywhere." She wasn't sure she *could* move.

Darting for the kitchen, Wes flung open the stove with an oven mitt already on and grabbed the pizza. The pan landed on top of the stove with a loud clank.

Bray watched him with amusement.

The kiss was magical—she could barely remember the other guy she had kissed. Bray didn't want to remember it either, because they had been drinking, and she did it all just to forget about Ruth. This … she didn't want to forget this moment.

Wes stood back in front of her and lifted a hand to her cheek. "I don't think it would've been a good idea to let the house burn down."

She giggled and pressed her lips softly to his, then moved

her mouth a hair's breadth from his ear, inhaling his clean scent from the shower. "No, it wouldn't have been, but I have a good idea now." She pressed her lips softly to his neck, just below his earlobe.

Wes's arms trailed down the sides to her lower back, tugging her closer against him. "What's the idea?"

"I'll show you," she hinted.

His mouth was on hers again, slow and sweet as she walked him down the hall. He knew the way without the slightest stumble, scuffing his feet backward until they were in his bedroom.

Wes's legs hit the bed, and he fell back, bringing her down on top of him. His hands moved to her face, the intensity of the kiss increasing. He tasted sweeter than anything she'd ever had, and a part of her wanted to kiss him forever, never losing the taste.

Bray's heartbeat sped up as his tongue slid into her mouth and tangled with hers. A soft moan escaped her when they rolled to the side. She wrapped a leg around his waist, pushing forward so his lower body was firmly on hers. He let out a deep groan when she rolled her hips forward.

She wasn't sure how far she wanted to take it, but she knew she wanted to feel more skin—*his skin*—against hers. Her fingertips grasped the edge of his shirt, and she lifted it up and over his head, tossing it on the carpet.

Bray didn't want to wait for him to take off her shirt, so she shucked it off herself. She felt his smile when her lips collided with his—in a secret wish, a solid hope, and a remarkable silent song that only they could hear. And they were both listening.

Reaching down in between them, Bray released the top button of his shorts and slid down the zipper.

His mouth pulled back from hers. "I don't know how far you want to take this, but we can't go all the way."

"Why not?" Even though she wanted more of him, she

didn't mind slowing down.

"I don't have a fucking condom," he groaned.

"So, you're scared of the rabies?" she joked and nipped his lower lip, running the tip of her tongue where her teeth had grazed him.

Wes drew her closer. "No, the babies. Luca is enough at the moment." He laughed and flipped her to her back. She didn't want any babies right then either.

"There are other things we could do," she said as she tugged on his shorts, and he kicked them to the floor.

"You want to show me? Or shall I show you?" he asked and pushed down her shorts.

Wes settled back between her legs, and *all of him* was perfectly there. His fingertips brushed her bare back as he undid the clasp of her bra. He then moved his lower body against hers in a delicious rhythm while cradling her breast.

As her body grew more heated from the friction, she needed something to happen. He must have sensed it, because his hand left her breast and drifted down between her legs. On instinct, she arched up toward him, and the kissing became sloppy and daring at the same time.

His hand slipped into her underwear, and she gasped when he started to rub the spot that yearned for it. The feeling built, and it built, and it built, until an uncontrollable ripple swept through her entire body. She couldn't stop from moaning Wes's name.

He smiled down at her, and said, "I'm glad I remembered what to do. It's been a while."

"Whatever." She giggled and let herself catch her breath for a moment, before flipping him to his back. "Your turn."

"You don't have to do anything." Wes stroked her braid and tickled her face with it.

"I've only been intimate with someone that one time, but I haven't done anything else—so I may be terrible at it." Bray wasn't entirely sure she knew what to do. And she didn't want to embarrass herself because she liked him so much.

"Hey." His voice was soft as he pulled her face to his and gave her a tender kiss. "It's with you, that's all that matters to me."

Bray grew braver as her fear vanished and let her fingers drift down to his boxers. She glided her hand inside, gripping him tight. A smile tugged at her lips, and just as Wes closed his eyes, the phone rang.

"*Of course*, the phone rings," he said tightly, still managing to semi-laugh it off as he reached to answer. "Hello?"

Bray rolled to her back, grinning as she stared up at the ceiling. Her chest was filled with happiness—more than in *The Goonies* when those kids found the ship of treasure.

Wes's face went from smiling to concerned as he listened. "Okay, that's fine. No problem. Is everything okay, though?" Bray continued to watch him as he concentrated on the conversation—she started to grow nervous. "Sure. Kyle can stay the night here. I'll wait for them outside."

Hanging up the phone, Wes turned to Bray, and slowly swallowed. "Something happened with Kyle's dad. He was attacked by some crazy woman and is in the hospital."

Bray didn't know what to think as she took a hard swallow, but she was worried. They hurriedly threw on their clothes and went to meet Luca and Kyle outside. The boys were already walking down the street toward them.

While Luca had a paint splatter of freckles sprinkled across his nose and cheeks, Kyle had an entire solar system of stars scattered across his face and arms. His red hair stood out like the orange of a sun going down for its nap as the moon awakened to rise. Bray wanted to pinch his round, squeezable cheeks, but she kept her hands to herself.

"Hey, you want to come in for some pizza? It may be a little cold, but I can heat it up for you." Wes asked the boys and gave Bray a sly look.

"I'm cool with eating it cold," Kyle said. He turned to Luca and whispered in his ear, "Dude your brother's girlfriend is *fine.*"

Luca scowled in disgust, and Wes attempted to hide his laugh. Bray wanted to pinch the kid's cheek even harder to get that thought out of his head.

After getting settled, the boys ate and played video games for a while before going to bed. A little before ten the phone rang, and when Wes answered, it was Kyle's Mom.

Throughout the entire conversation, Wes's brows went up and down. He said "uh huh" numerous times with his mouth opening and closing—very fish-like. Robotically, he hung up the phone and turned to Bray.

"What happened?" she asked, concern filling up her entire body.

Wes shook his head and ran a hand through his thick hair. "The attack happened when Kyle's dad left work and was heading to his truck. He saw a woman who he thought needed money approaching him, and he reached into his pocket to pull out some cash to give her. Instead of taking the money, the woman ran at Kyle's dad and knocked him to the ground. He managed to push her off, but she was strong and she… She bit his ear off."

Bray's eyes opened as wide as they could go. "She *what*? Like she ate it?" She couldn't comprehend what he had just said.

"No, she spit it out. When security came, she was raging and completely out of control, trying to either push his eye in or yank it out. The cop was going to arrest her, but then she attacked him, too—and bit his shoulder. Somehow after shoving her off, the cop shot her in the leg to slow her, but she kept coming at him, so he had to shoot her down."

"How's Kyle's dad now?" Bray didn't want to think about how scared Kyle was going to be when he found out. She was shaken from just hearing about it.

"They're reattaching his ear. So, there's that… He's going

to be okay, though.”

“Thank goodness.” Her shoulders relaxed, and she sighed in relief.

Wes rubbed his bottom lip back and forth against his front teeth.

“What else?” she asked hesitantly.

“The body was shot twice, and there was no blood. This is the third person who has gone insane, attacked people, and then get shot and killed. To top it all off, no blood can be found in the body. How’s that possible? And better yet: what is going on?” Wes’s face grew grim, and Bray’s heart sunk because she couldn’t uncover an answer either.

“I don’t know. Your world is so different than mine. Laith isn’t as clear to me now, but something like this wouldn’t be so farfetched there. Here though … something like this shouldn’t be happening.”

He let out a heavy breath and took a seat on the couch. “You’re right. It shouldn’t.”

Bray sat down beside him and pulled his hand into hers, interlacing their fingers. “I might not know what’s going on, but maybe I can try to figure something out. I don’t know how, though.”

“We just won’t think about it tonight.” He stared at their interlaced fingers with an unreadable expression. “About earlier, I…”

She wondered if Wes regretted what had happened between them, and if she should let go of his hand. Bray released it and placed her palm on top of her knee, rubbing her thumb in slow circles against the skin. “Yes?” Her breathing drew in shakily.

“I liked it.” He smiled.

And her breath came out steadily. “Me, too.”

Wrapping his strong arm around Bray’s shoulders, Wes tugged her to his chest, and they sat like that together in silence for a while.

Bray worried that Brenik was still gone. If something

happened to him like what had happened to Kyle's dad, she would be heartbroken. Brenik would be able to escape an attack easily since he could just fly off, but she was still nervous about him not being back yet.

Then there was this thing between her and Wes. She knew she was being selfish to Brenik by staying this size—living a life that wasn't in a tree hole.

"What are you thinking about?" Wes asked.

"I guess I won't be able to sleep in the tree since Kyle's staying the night."

"Nope."

"Couch?" She quietly patted the back of the cushion.

"Nope."

"The car?" She stood up like she was going to walk out the front door.

"Nope." He wiggled his finger at her to follow him to his room.

Bray rubbed her chin like she was thinking hard about it, then shrugged and let him lead the way.

They both sat on the bed after Wes closed the door behind them. "Since we can't do anything now that Luca has a friend over, there's only going to be cuddling tonight." He smiled, then leaned over and whispered, "And maybe a kiss or two."

Bray softly patted his shoulder. "What about shoulder time? I like sleeping on your shoulder."

"More than Luca's?" He grinned.

Bray cocked her head as if in thought. "That's a hard question. He does read me stories."

"You can stay this size tonight, so I can be your favorite cuddle partner."

"I'm willing to try this. I've never had a cuddle partner before," she murmured.

"You've been missing out, then. But kissing partner sounds better." Wrapping his arms around her, Wes pressed his mouth against hers and lowered them both down to the mattress. They kissed for a little while without anything growing too heated. It was sweet and gentle.

When their lips separated, Wes rolled to his back and she nestled her head on his chest, folding her arm around his stomach.

She felt lit up, brighter than the moon and all the stars combined.

Eighteen

Brenik

Brenik was ready for his night with Rana. The homeless woman from two nights before had satisfied his hunger, for now. He felt like such a selfish prick—there had to be another way.

Throwing on a pair of jeans and a T-shirt, he headed for the elementary school. On the way there, it gave him time to think about things. Talking to Bray was still an issue, and he decided he would do it over the weekend. He would even apologize for how he had been over the years, growing green with envy about her luck—when he should have been happy for her. To her, he would confess all the parts of himself that needed to be unloaded.

On his left, he passed a neat line of pier and beam homes before finally seeing the brick school building.

The dials on his watch showed him it was three o'clock—five minutes until the bell rang. Rows of cars already lined up around the curving curbside. Turning away from them, Brenik walked to the front of the building and stood away from the other adults who were waiting for their kids.

A loud buzz came from the speakers which must have been the poorly sounding release bell. Kids of all sizes ran out of the building, and Brenik stepped out of the way, weirded out from all the creepiness.

He had seen kids plenty of times, but never in such a close proximity to where they were surrounding him. Claustrophobia seemed to be setting in. He was unsure about the situation—they were so much smaller.

Two boys were walking out of the building—one redheaded and the other had dark hair. The one with dark hair lifted his head and looked at Brenik, his eyes squinting in confusion.

The dark-haired boy said bye to his friend and wandered in Brenik's direction. Brenik turned his head to avoid the strange kid's stare and pretended to rub at his eye.

"Hey," the kid said, stepping a little too close for Brenik's comfort.

"Hello," Brenik replied flatly, glancing away.

"You look like my friend."

He gave the kid a hard stare. "Sorry, I don't have red hair."

The nuisance adjusted his backpack on his shoulder. "No, not that one, my other one."

"Look, kid, before this gets odd, you better go." Brenik didn't need some parent thinking he was trying to steal the child.

The boy's eyes searched Brenik's face to the point where he felt uncomfortable. "You have the same pale blue eyes and jet-black hair as her, but it's not just that... You're *him*, aren't you?"

Whoever the kid was, he was starting to annoy the fuck out of him. "No, I'm not."

"Brenik?" the kid asked.

Brenik's eyes widened. He grabbed the kid's arm a little too tightly and pulled him to the wall. "How do you know my name?" He had no earthly idea how this boy would know it.

The kid flicked Brenik's hand away from his arm. "Because you're Bray's brother." This kid... This kid was the same one who he had seen through the window. He hadn't paid very close attention to his face, but the hair and body matched.

"You're living in Ruth's old house?" Brenik asked.

Not frightened in the slightest it seemed, the kid tilted his head to the side, like Brenik should already have known this. And he probably should have. "Yeah, me and my brother, and now Bray."

"She's inside your house?" Brenik was confused as to why Bray would be in his house.

"Yeah, she's been waiting for you to come back. Also, she said you couldn't change forms, so how are you like this?" The boy's finger wiggled up and down at Brenik's body, and he wanted to snap it off.

"This isn't the place to talk about such things. Listen, kid, can you keep quiet about this for a few days? I'll come by over the weekend." He was going to chew Bray out for whatever was going on here.

"I'll give you two days, since Bray's my friend," the kid said, holding up two fingers.

Brenik wanted to shove the kid away, but he nodded instead. *Fucking Bray*, apparently parading her secrets to the whole world.

"You know Luca?" Rana asked from behind them, causing Brenik to straighten with a jerk. He hoped she hadn't heard any of their conversation.

"Hello, Miss Alvi, this is my brother's girlfriend's brother," Luca said sweetly.

Brother's girlfriend? Brenik's brow furrowed in confusion, and Luca gave him a smirk. Brenik needed to get away from the kid before he blew a fuse.

Rana turned to Brenik and smiled. "I didn't know you had a sister."

"A twin sister actually," Luca piped in. Brenik wanted this kid to zip it up already.

"I wonder if she looks like you, Brenik."

"She does." Luca nodded one too many times.

"See you this weekend, *Luca*," Brenik said with a flat tone, clenching his teeth a little too tightly, trying to get the kid to go away.

"Two days." Luca hinted at their deal as he walked off, holding up two fingers again. Then he yelled, "Bye, Miss Alvi."

Finally, the kid rounded the corner, and Brenik turned to Rana when she said, "He's one of the sweetest kids in my class—and brightest, too."

Of course he is. His blood boiled as he thought about how stupid Bray could be. Trusting Ruth was one thing because she was older and nurturing, but he didn't trust that kid—not one bit. It didn't bother Brenik that Bray was walking around in her human form, since he was mostly human now, too. But the fact that he didn't know those people bothered him.

"What do you want to do now?" he asked, changing the subject. Rana was wearing a long skirt with a green blouse tucked in, pulling off the teacher look extremely well.

"We could go to the movies, and then maybe go to your place?" Brenik wished she would have said to go straight to his place but going to the movies would be better than throwing up shit at a restaurant again.

The last time he had gone to the movie theater, he and Bray were stuffed inside Ruth's purse. It had been an early showtime for a movie that had been out a while, so they were the only ones in the theater. Nostalgia was a combination of good and bad for him, so he shut down that memory.

"I'm cool with that. I'll even let you pick the movie." Brenik grinned as he grabbed her hand. Rana intertwined their fingers and led him in the direction of her car.

"You have to admit the movie was ridiculous," Brenik said as he held the exit door of the movie theater open for Rana.

"What do you mean? It was beautiful." Rana let out a long, adoring sigh.

Brenik had let Rana choose the movie, and that had been a mistake. The movie poster for *Powder* had looked terrible to begin with, but there was nothing in particular he really wanted to see.

"The ending made no damn sense." He was still confused as fuck as to what had even happened to the main character, Powder, in the film, and he had seen some disturbing shit in his life.

Rana gave him a light shove. "Do we need to watch it again?"

"No. Next time I'll choose what to watch."

"Deal." She stood on the tip of her toes and kissed his cheek, making sitting through the shitty movie worth it.

Once they got back to Brenik's place, he offered her a drink. "Soda?"

"Sure."

He had gone to the store earlier to purchase some food and drinks for Rana in case she needed something. But he wouldn't be eating.

Grabbing Rana a Sprite, Brenik plopped down beside her on the couch. "Do you still talk to your parents? You told me when we first met that you didn't get along because of how strict they were." He wanted to know everything about this woman.

Her expression faltered, and Brenik felt terrible for bringing it up. "Not at the moment. Their beliefs are so strong—which is great for them—but I'm still trying to find myself and what to believe in." She paused. "My parents and I even had an argument over Mexican food because they wanted chicken curry."

Disgust crossed Brenik's face as if he smelled something

bad. "If it was Maria's, I understand the argument."

She swatted his arm but didn't appear upset any longer. "Just because you had one bad experience at Maria's doesn't mean it's bad. I didn't get sick from the meal."

It wasn't Maria's fault for him getting sick—it was the curse that was a prayer answered and a demon burning him alive. Light and dark would continue to battle inside of him for as long as he chose.

"Do you want to show me the rest of your place?" She craned her neck, happy to explore.

He led her to his room and pointed at the bed against one wall, then the wooden dresser on the opposite side. "This is it."

"Let me know if you need help dressing up the place, but I like it," Rana said as she walked over to the dresser. "Is this one of your paintings?" She reached for the portrait, and Brenik ran to her, tearing her arm away from it.

She frowned down at his hand. Brenik realized he was gripping her wrist a little too tightly, and he dropped it like it had electrocuted him. "Sorry, it's just that one is important to me. My grandmother painted it last year before she died," he lied, but not faking the distressed lines on his face.

"Oh, she was an artist, too?" Rana's lips parted in interest.

"Yeah, she would work on her art almost every day," he answered. Not really a lie since Ruth did sew all the time, and sewing could be considered an art form.

"Show me something of yours." At that moment, Brenik knew he shouldn't have told her he was trying to be an artist.

"Everything is still at my sister's place since she has extra room." Rana wasn't dumb, so he hurried on. "But I can bring some here next time you come over." He didn't think it would be too hard to get some paint, throw it around on some canvases and call it "abstract" art.

Needing to find a distraction before she started asking more questions about his life, Brenik took a step closer to her. "You smell good." The scent was fresh, like spearmint.

Rana rolled her eyes. "Is that supposed to be a pickup line?"

He stepped even closer. "Possibly?" She didn't roll her eyes at him that time.

Moving a lock of hair behind her ear, Brenik leaned forward to her neck and inhaled. The minty aroma became infectious, and he swiped the tip of his tongue right below her ear.

Slowly, Brenik licked his way across and up under her jaw until he was at her lips. Then he pulled her hips against his.

"With anyone else, I would find this incredibly strange, but I'm finding this rather intoxicating," Rana murmured.

He responded by pressing his lips delicately against hers, then he echoed the gesture to both her eyes and the center of her forehead.

Rana kept her eyes shut as Brenik kissed his way from her forehead, down her nose, and right to her red lipstick-stained lips.

The heart inside his chest was unwinding like a miniature yo-yo, achingly similar to the one he once had back at Ruth's. It bounced up and down inside his chest, knocking every other organ out of the way to stay front and center as it reached toward the other heart buried beneath Rana's rib cage.

Brenik kissed her slowly, dragging his hand up to Rana's chest to feel her heartbeat, but clothes were in the way. He reached down to grab the edge of her shirt and hauled it up and over her head.

Taking a step near the bed with his arms around her, Brenik gently unclasped Rana's lacy black bra. He kissed his way down one shoulder as he lowered the strap, then repeated his movements on the other side, until he discarded the bra on the floor.

Delicately, Brenik slid his hand from her stomach to the valley in between her breasts. There, he sensed the thump of her heart—felt it, heard it, saw it, adored it. He ignored all the viciousness inside himself and moved his hand to her breast, squeezing it with the right amount of pressure that had her moaning.

The rest of their clothing came off, then she pressed him down on the bed. He rolled them to her back, kissing his way down Rana's body, then up to her mouth where her lipstick was now smeared between him and her.

Even though he hadn't done this before, his mating instinct took over. He may have appeared human, but he would never be one.

"Are you sure you want to?" he asked, trying to keep his voice steady. If she wasn't ready he could wait, but he would head straight into the bathroom and take care of his issue. He wouldn't be able to contain himself.

"I'm sure." In the low lighting, Brenik realized that Rana's brown eyes were flecked with gold. The tiny discovery about her had him feeling more for her than he already was. Her small mole was waiting for him to kiss, which he did before caressing her lips once more.

Brenik slid into her, then paused to catch his breath, before beginning to move. He was going to fall in love with her—he just knew it.

He started slowly, getting the right rhythm, then increased his pace. Their kisses became wild with frantic fury. Something, *something* was coming over him, and on instinct he moved down to her neck, breathing in her natural scent mixed with mint.

She moaned again as his tongue and lips covered the sensitive area. Just one taste. Just one quick taste to see what pumped through the throbbing vein hidden under her smooth brown skin. He couldn't—he shouldn't—he didn't want to— but he did. He fought to control the inner demon, but it was inevitable.

His fangs lowered and brushed against her skin. She seemed to like it, so he pushed his teeth down until the scent of blood caressed his nostrils and the thick liquid flowed upward.

She let out a soft cracked sound, and he started to pull himself out of his disillusioned state. He was fighting it, desperately. But then she dragged him closer, and he could do nothing except surrender to his deepest desire. While continuing to move in her, he bent his head back down and fed. From the sound of Rana's moans, she was enjoying it as much as he was.

The taste was the sweetest and most delicious thing he had ever had in his life, lusher than any fruit. The world grew into a ribbon of color when his body trembled from being inside Rana, along with the blood that festered within his mouth— the perfect blend of ecstasy.

Brenik's head cleared, no longer dizzy.

Guilt hit him as he swallowed the blood, unsure of how he would explain that part to her. Brenik decided he would reveal the truth and figure it all out with her, because she deserved to know.

As he brought his head up above hers, heart pounding, he stilled. No movement. Rana's eyes were lifeless as she stared at the ceiling, her face pale.

She was dead.

And he had killed her.

Nineteen

Brenik

"No!" Brenik roared as he lifted Rana's dead shoulders like some kind of doll. Setting her softly back down, he spat out the taste of blood that remained in his mouth.

"How could I have done this?" he whispered. "Not her. Not *her*." Gripping the dresser, he slammed it to the floor—the painting hit the wood and landed in pristine condition.

Brenik searched around the room, not knowing what he was looking for, but he didn't want the blood. He didn't want *her* blood inside him anymore. Sticking his finger down his throat, Brenik made himself heave. Most of it splattered out, not black, but fresh and crimson—still warm from being inside of him.

The portrait on the wooden floor stared back at him. Brenik refused to put Rana's blood on it—he would rather wither away that second.

Plastering his palms on the sides of his head, he couldn't think—he couldn't think about anything except for what he had just done. He sobbed desolately, all hope lost, and dropped to his knees, hands pressed against the floor, slapping it and yelling as spittle plummeted from his mouth to the wood. Eventually, he couldn't take the pain anymore, and he cried himself to sleep.

Help, the first word he thought when he woke. Brenik needed Bray. She was the only one who would understand.

Brenik hurried and threw on his clothing. Struggling with his emotions, he then put Rana's skirt and top back on. He didn't want to leave her naked, like she was some piece of trash. She wasn't like the others.

It didn't take him long to reach the tree—his real *home*. Brenik scurried up the thick branches like his life depended on it—and it did.

"Bray," he hollered, not caring who heard him. "Bray, *please*." She wasn't there. He stuck his hand inside the hole and slapped the bottom, destroying their things in the process. He didn't care. Brenik hated to admit it to himself, but he did need her—he always had.

Tears flowed down his cheeks as he climbed back down, falling to the ground in a pathetic ball. A door creaked open. When he looked up, sunlight highlighted his sister, and he cried harder, unsure if it was from relief or anger.

Without shutting the door, Bray ran toward him. "Brenik? What's wrong?" Bray asked frantically as she helped him to sit on the ground. He threw his arms around her, crying even harder.

"I screwed up, Bray. I've screwed up so badly. I need help, please," he begged.

Unwrapping her arms from around Brenik, Bray pulled back and scanned him over, her jaw dropping down all the way. "How? How are you like this?"

Brenik told her. He told her every detail: about his envy, about not wanting to wither and die in the tree hole, going to the Stone of Desire, the curse he accepted without knowing the consequences. Then the deaths he had caused—Jeremy, the homeless people, and Rana. How he hadn't wanted to do these things yet struggled to resist. How it was all a never-ending necessity that was beyond his control.

Bray barely looked at him, her face hard and furious. She kept glancing back at the house.

Brenik stared at the open door. "Where are they? I met the kid yesterday at school. He told me most of it."

Her lips parted, and her brows shot up. "Luca?"

He nodded.

"Wes took Luca with him to do a job for work." Bray lifted Brenik's chin. "Take me to her."

"Okay," Brenik whispered. Slowly, he stood from the ground, wiping away the last of his tears.

Something changed in Bray's expression, like she had discovered something. "You know, I think the bodies are coming back to life because of this. But they are dangerous. One attacked me at the park and another… Another bit off the ear of a man down the street," she seethed.

Cringing, Brenik nodded because he knew what was going on. "I didn't know that would happen when I first started. But when I found out, I still couldn't bring myself to stop."

"So, you decided to choose homeless people, Brenik?" Bray grimaced. He opened his mouth to respond, but she stopped him. "Let me guess, you thought by killing people in the park that don't really have a life, you were some sort of savior? Is that it? How do you know those people wouldn't have had a turnaround? Kyle's dad could have died because of the crazy attacker. *I* could have died. Doesn't that bother you?"

"Of course it does, Bray! You don't understand. You aren't in my head. You never have been. I couldn't—*can't*—control what goes on in this messed up place of mine," Brenik spat. He sure didn't think he was anyone's savior.

"You shouldn't have struck a deal with the Stone, and you should have come to me right away." There was nothing Bray could have done. He still would have been in the same miserable position, but now he would give anything to go back into the past.

"You're one to talk, you chose to have a gift without knowing what it was," he pointed out.

"Brenik, I was ten. I would have trusted any Disney villain offering me something." She sighed. "But if I was in your position, who knows what I would have accepted." Bray changed the subject. "Has she woken yet?"

"What? She's *dead*." Bitterness laced his words.

Bray frowned at him. "I know, but eventually she will awaken like the others did, right?"

His chest tightened—that hadn't even crossed his mind. "I'm not sure." He didn't know if she would, but after what Bray told him had happened to his victims, he was afraid of what might occur if Rana did.

"We'll take her to the Stone and see if we can fix all this together, all right?" Bray insisted.

Brenik nodded, even though he didn't want to see that fucker again.

Their walk to the forest was accompanied by silence, until they reached the cabin. "You've actually been staying here?" Bray asked, staring at his temporary home.

"Yes." He was already sick of her questions.

"What did you plan to do when the owner came back?" That was actually a good question that he had no answer to.

"I didn't think that far ahead, Bray."

"You never do." And she was right, but he didn't say anything as they approached the front porch. Brenik held the door open for Bray and led her to his room.

His jaw tightened when he saw Rana sprawled across the bed—for a second he thought she would have been gone, or maybe even awakened into one of those things. But she lay there just the same, except her skin was more pale than brown. He shut his eyes and held them as tight as he could to not let any tears slip out, before opening them back up.

Bray covered her mouth with her hand, but he knew she tried to stay strong as she was faced with Rana's dead body. They had seen dead things—more mutilated than not—all the time when they were younger in Laith, so they had to grow a thicker skin.

"You didn't say the painting was a portrait of yourself," Bray said as she lowered her hand from her mouth and toed the edge of the canvas.

He shrugged. "Does it matter?"

"It's very Dorian Grayish—don't you think?" She rubbed her lower lip with her index and middle finger, staring back and forth between him and the portrait.

His brow furrowed as he studied the painting. "I don't know what that is."

"That's because you never read books."

"That's because I *can't* read books," he growled with frustration. She already knew that.

Bray held her hands up in front of herself. "I know you can't. I'm only stating the fact, little brother."

Slumping his shoulders, Brenik murmured, "Let's just hurry and see if the Stone will awaken to help us."

Carefully, he gathered Rana's stiff body in his arms and held her like a piece of fragile glass. Brenik was worried she would wake up like the others, yet happy if she woke up at all.

Carrying a dead body couldn't be labeled as anything other than suspicious, so Brenik and Bray hurried through the forest as far away from sight as they could.

His head filled with images he wanted to hammer away. Maybe he could ask the Stone to reverse time, and he would never leave the tree hole again—then Rana and the others would still be alive.

They were close, the Stone almost in sight, when Brenik felt a small twitch against his chest. Thrill and nervousness rebounded through him. When Rana's eyes flicked open with murder, he was ready for her.

Snarling, she slashed his face with her fingernails. And Brenik let her as he ran the rest of the way, passing Bray who was yelling for him to stop. She called out that she would help him. But help him *how?* She wasn't strong enough to keep Rana still.

A white outline angled into his line of sight, and Brenik dashed straight for it, ignoring the pain from the scratches across his cheek.

When Brenik reached the Stone, he tried to set Rana down gently on the ground, but she was already starting to run away.

"Flip her over for now," Bray panted, out of breath from trying to catch up with Brenik.

Rana hadn't gained all her strength back, but she grew stronger by the second. Turning her over, Brenik looked at Bray and said, "Now what?"

"Bind her hands with your shirt." Bray sat on top of Rana, attempting to hold her down.

Ripping his shirt over his head, Brenik motioned Bray away, and pulled Rana's hands behind her back to tie them together. He hated everything about it. Bray seemed to hate it even more as she watched on.

Bray took off her over shirt, leaving on her tank top, and handed the fabric to Brenik to bind Rana's ankles together.

Rana bared her teeth, furiously grunting, and something inside Brenik cracked at the sight. He was going to fix this—he owed it to her. Brenik ran toward the Stone and slapped his hand on top of it. Bray placed hers calmly next to his, and they waited.

Nothing happened. He should have known. "Please," he pleaded.

In answer, the ground shook beneath their feet, the trees vibrating. Relieved, Brenik's chin fell to his chest, and he stepped away from the Stone, next to where Bray had moved.

With his heart anxiously pounding, he watched the same

routine of the Stone's arms and legs sprouting from the rock. Lastly, the alabaster head with the unreadable black eyes protruded forward. Brenik wished he could know what went on inside the head of the creature who answered desires but would cost one dearly.

"What do you desire?" the Stone boomed inside his head. "I have already granted your wishes."

"It isn't for me—it's for her." Brenik pointed desperately to Rana. She was no longer moving, but watching the Stone with a sharpness so deep, he wasn't sure if she was going to try and attack it.

"Ah. What do you think she desires?" the Stone asked.

"To live—to not be like this... Make her like she was—take back what you gave me, but please, help her." He would do anything—*anything*.

"I cannot reverse what I gave to you, but I can change her current state."

Bray watched on blankly, and Brenik dropped to his knees in mercy.

"Bring her to me," the Stone demanded.

He nodded and shakily lifted Rana in his arms. She wriggled desperately, but he ignored her struggles, setting her down onto the Stone's open palm and backing away.

The large hand closed around Rana until it was set into a closed fist. Slowly, its digits unraveled like a flower in spring, opening for the world to see its beauty.

Rana was still there when Brenik stepped closer. He scooped her still body out of the Stone's palm and held his thumb under her nose. No breaths.

"She isn't breathing!" he cried, his shoulders drooping as he held Rana tightly.

"It was the only way to save her," the Stone answered, its head lowering to Brenik's.

"You didn't save her. You killed her," Brenik accused. He wanted to break the stone into a thousand pieces and throw them all into the deepest depths of the ocean.

"Her soul was already gone. You waited too long." The Stone's eyes seemed to accuse Brenik of his own wrongdoing. It was Brenik's fault.

"You mean, I could have come here right after it happened?"

"Yes." The short answer burned a slow and gaping hole into Brenik's chest as he realized he could have saved Rana's life.

The Stone started to pull himself back into its rock form, when Brenik took a step forward and begged, "Fix me."

"I told you, you chose what you chose." Then the Stone folded back into the shape of a rose.

Brenik roared as his whole world came crashing down around him. Setting down Rana's body, he ran toward the Stone and pounded his fists against the hardness, trying to crack it in half. Something yanked him back, and he turned around to unleash his anger on it—on Bray.

"Go away, Bray," he warned.

Without the tiniest flinch, Bray stood her ground. "No."

"I said, Go. The *fuck*. Away!" Brenik didn't want anyone around him, and he didn't want Bray to see him like this.

She took a step toward him, her arms crossed. "I'm not leaving."

Brenik bent down to Rana's body and untied her wrists and ankles. He tossed the shirts aside and reached down to lightly touch Rana's back. Her body turned to a sand-like substance and dissolved into the ground, becoming part of the earth. Brenik stared at the dirt in horror. The Stone didn't only kill what was inside her, but it had taken her body, too.

Bray moved next to him, eyes wide, looking equally afraid, but Brenik knew she tried to hide her terror behind pursed lips. "It's—it's better this way," she said. "No one can cut up her body trying to find answers, like they have with the other victims. It will be okay, Brenik."

He couldn't lift his eyes from the ground as he whispered,

"How will it ever be okay, Bray? I kill people. I kill people to stay young. Even when I don't try to kill people, I still do."

"Then don't do it anymore. Grow old with me." She didn't understand. There were times when the hunger was uncontrollable, and he had to give into it—he had *wanted* to give into it.

"Just leave me alone for a little while, and I will come by tomorrow. I have to think about things." Brenik ran his hands through his hair, squeezing it fiercely.

Bray's eyes narrowed at Brenik like she could read everything in his head. "Right, but I'll come with you."

He didn't want her to come—he wanted to be by himself, with his thoughts. "I *need* to be alone."

"Are you sure, Brenik? If you don't stop by, I will have to come and find you." He could tell she was worried and maybe a bit frightened.

"Bray, go home. I will come by tomorrow. I promise."

"You're going to need help, and I'm going to help you stop this." Brenik knew she would try, but he wasn't sure if he wanted anyone's help. He would rather do it himself.

"I love you, Bray. I will be okay." He had never told her that, no matter how many times she had spoken the words to him. There were times he had felt he should never say the words aloud because sometimes he hated her, too, but this time the love won out.

"I love you, too, little brother," she said, wrapping her arms around him, her eyes filling with tears. He wanted to cry and scream like a child for her to stop, but he slung his arms around her, holding her tight.

After she left the forest, Brenik fell to the ground where Rana had once lain and curled into himself. He had lied to Bray. He wasn't going to be okay—he would never be okay.

Twenty

Bray

Bray was shaken after she left Brenik, but she knew she had to leave him alone. Her hands quivered as she exited the forest and crossed the pavement. The same road where she had once almost been struck by a car—if it hadn't been for Brenik, who had pulled her back from the brink of death.

Her brother was no longer a bat, but he wasn't human either. Brenik was something far worse, yet he was still him. Bray felt that maybe she shouldn't have left him there. The things he had done... In this world he would be arrested for it, and in her world, there was no consequence for wrongdoing. Both aspects pulled at her conscience. She thought about the jovkins who had murdered her kind without repercussion.

Wes's car was already parked in the driveway, and she didn't know what to do or say to him. She rang the doorbell, unable to erase the image of Rana out of her mind, or the fact that the Stone said it could have saved her. Rana had just turned. If only Bray had gone straight there with Brenik, instead of making him tell her the whole story of his new life.

Luca swung open the door. "We were worried about you."

"I know I promised I would leave you a note, Luca, but my brother showed up." She hardened her gaze a little as she looked down at him—his eyes were ticking side to side.

"You know I saw him at school, then? With Miss Alvi?" Luca's body wiggled and squirmed with nervousness. "He asked me not to tell you, and I told him I would give him two days. It hasn't been that long yet."

Bray swept Luca's bangs away from his brow and patted his head. "I know, little beast, I know." She couldn't be mad at him. "Where's Wes? I need to talk to him for a few minutes."

Luca's head motioned at the back door. "He's in the backyard again, doing something with the plants. I think he said something about outlining it with stone, so he's trying to get an estimation of how many rocks he needs."

"I'll be back there, then." Bray brushed past Luca, then turned her head over her shoulder. "Maybe we can watch a movie later, or better yet, read me a story? Maybe *Alice's Adventures in Wonderland* this time?" she asked, putting on the bravest act she could. But she could tell Luca knew something wasn't right when he nodded, his fingers fidgeting.

Bray left and found Wes working on the garden—he lifted his head in her direction and gave her a smile. "Glad you're back. You can come over here and help me real quick."

"You seem to be handling the garden well all by yourself," Bray said mischievously as she approached him.

Wes let the yellow measuring tape slide back into its container. "Maybe it's just a reason to get you over here."

The expression on her face faltered.

"What's wrong?" Wes asked, setting down the measuring tape.

"I was with Brenik." Bray knew she probably shouldn't say anything because she loved her brother so much. But with everything he had done, it would be wrong to keep it from Wes. She didn't want to break this special thing that was blossoming between them.

"Your brother?"

"Yes. Listen. I—uh—have something to tell you," Bray stuttered.

Wes's back straightened and his lips thinned. "Are you leaving?"

"No, it's not that. He's supposed to come by the house, possibly tomorrow." Bray wasn't sure if he would really show up, or if she would have to hunt him down.

"He does live in the tree, right?" Wes glanced up toward the tree hole.

"So… He's not small anymore," Bray mumbled, tapping the ends of her fingers together.

His brows both lowered, and a deep line settled between them. "Okay, so he's like you now?" *Close, but not quite.*

"Not exactly. He, um … went to the Stone of Desire and it granted him his wish to become human. But it came with a price. Brenik had this fear of withering and growing old like Ruth, so his desire was to stay young, not just to become human. To stop him from progressing in age naturally, there is a terrible hunger he must live with if he wants to stay young. That's how I understand it, anyway."

Wes shook his head with his face scrunched up. "Wait, I'm completely confused here. So he's going to live forever?"

"I don't know! But you know the four people that had holes in their necks without blood?" Bray asked.

"No, I forgot about that," he said sarcastically. "But you mean three people, right?"

"No, I mean four," Bray started. "Brenik can only feed off human blood. He has this painting that he presses the blood onto, and it absorbs it in order for him to stay young." She tried to make the sentence sound like an everyday occurrence.

Wes's eyes widened, and he didn't blink for a long while. The bout of silence between them seemed unnaturally long. "Your brother is a vampire." Not a question, only a statement.

"No, he isn't a vampire." She wouldn't say he was a vampire, *per se.*

He flung his hands up. "I'm sorry—he's going around drinking people's blood when he's hungry? That sounds like a vampire to me. Not to mention the weird immortality thing." His hands continued to hover in the air.

"Brenik's not a vampire—he can go out in the sun. He isn't immortal if he doesn't drink the blood." Bray grimaced.

"This is just like the whole bat argument. I let that one go, but I'm right this time. He's some type of damn vampire. I don't care what you say. Are you forgetting that his victims have been roaming around attacking people?" Wes was angry, and she was, too, but Brenik was still her brother.

"From what the Stone said earlier, Brenik could have saved his victims before they awoke again." She didn't mention that Brenik had carried the dead body of a woman he was involved with through the forest to find answers. It wasn't going to solve anything right then.

"That doesn't even begin to counter the fact of what he's done. Look at Kyle's dad! And what am I supposed to do? Do I call the cops and tell them that these victims have a case of vampiric rabies, because a bat turned vampire is going around murdering them because he's *hungry?*" Wes's eyes bulged, and the veins on the sides of his neck throbbed.

"This situation isn't as strange to me because of where I'm from. And I'm not saying it's okay. It's far from okay, but I think I can fix him. If I can't, then I'll think about what I can do after. Just give me a week." Bray had to try, or she would never forgive herself.

Wes sighed. "A lot can happen in a week, Bray."

"I know. Let me try talking to the Stone one more time—if it will listen."

"Let me come with you, then." He was already moving toward her, but it was her mistake to correct. She couldn't help but blame herself.

"I don't know if it will awaken if you're there, but I'll tell you everything when I come back." Without another word,

Bray left. She could have changed and flown, but she wanted to walk and absorb the situation. The pit in her stomach was growing, an endless bottom of a sea covered in a whirlwind of darkness.

She thought about all the choices she had made. Maybe she should have stayed in Laith. They had been hiding just as much here as they had been there. But here, no one could smell them out to rip them apart and eat.

Bray wandered the rest of the way with a blank mind as she approached the Stone. It sat there as if it had never been roused before.

Shakily, she reached forward and pressed her hand on top, begging the Stone to talk to her. Bray was willing to sacrifice herself for her brother if she had to. "Please talk to me. Take what you gave me. Take my gift and give it to Brenik." The Stone didn't budge.

She sobbed quietly against the rough surface when a light rustle disrupted her crying. "Who's there?" she shouted, wiping the tears away from her face. "Brenik?"

A small form stepped out from behind a tree. "Luca? What are you doing here?"

His shoulders slumped. "I heard your conversation with Wes."

"How? Weren't you inside?" Bray hadn't heard or seen him out there.

"I went out the front and hid behind the gate," he explained. She didn't have enough energy to stir up any anger about his eavesdropping.

"Something happened to Miss Alvi, didn't it?" Luca asked, his face falling into sadness.

"Why would you think that?" Bray didn't want to break the news to Luca.

"Because I heard you say four people, and Brenik was with Miss Alvi yesterday." Bray wasn't sure whether to tell Luca the truth or not. He was a ten-year-old boy—a human boy. He was at an age where he was still innocent yet approaching the level of growing up. But he had done a lot of growing up already, and Bray had to learn about life the hard way right after she was born. He could handle it.

"Yes, Luca. Miss Alvi is gone."

With a heavy sigh, he nodded, and Bray wrapped her arms around him. She wouldn't tell him not to worry because she was worried herself.

Luca backed away from her, blinking away tears. Then he shrugged a shoulder and tilted his head at it. "You want a ride home?"

She didn't have the strength to tell him no, and their house wasn't far anyway. "You read my mind." Bray transformed, and the long blades of grass rubbed at her. Luca bent down to scoop her up and plopped her onto his shoulder.

"Wes is going to be so mad that I didn't tell him I left." He had a look on his face that appeared sorry, even though he wasn't.

"Luca!" Bray scolded.

"I'm just kidding. You know he's still in the garden—he probably doesn't even know I'm gone." She highly doubted that.

Bray tapped the edge of his shoulder. "Don't ever do that again without telling Wes, okay?"

"Okay." Luca nodded in agreement.

When they got to their street, he pulled Bray from his shoulder and held her close to his chest as he ran the rest of the way home. She bobbled and her stomach churned, but she enjoyed the wind brushing against her face.

Luca opened the front door and released her in the air. She changed forms, and they headed to the back door.

Wes glanced up from the garden, his hands covered in specks of dirt. "You're back. I was about to go on a search mission."

Luca shut the door behind her to stay inside, while smiling

deviously since he got away with his crime.

Wes grabbed three of the four lawn chairs, leaning against the back of the house. He propped the chairs open in the middle of the yard for them to sit. Bray sat down next to him, and the other one was open in case Luca wanted to venture back outside. Wes could be so thoughtful.

Without a word, he dropped his hand down in between them and wiggled his fingers. Fighting a smile, she took his hand and leaned back to think about anything except what was really going on. There were a lot of times when Bray had gotten her and Brenik in trouble. It was her fault now, just as it was then.

"Look, Brenik, I found the biggest pear up here. If you help me get it down, I will share more than half with you," Bray said, tugging on the fruit that wouldn't budge.

"I do not know about this, Bray. We are supposed to be extra quiet when we venture out this far. Junah does not want us to come out here without her, remember?" Brenik replied, flapping his wings and soaring up beside Bray.

Bray had begged Brenik to come with her—he had wanted them to stay home. She was worried about what Junah would say, but she wanted to retrieve the pear for Brenik, and a little for herself. They had been craving the fruit for a long time and there were no pear trees anywhere near Junah's part of the forest.

Reaching toward the thin stem, she tugged on the fruit again and hoped it would drop. Brenik shook his head and sighed, grasping the pear in his grip. "Okay, on the count of three we will both tug. One, two..." Bray had already begun to tug because she could not wait. "Three."

The tree branch rustled loudly as Brenik pushed down. "What is in this pear?" he asked, his voice tight.

"Goodness!" Bray squealed, pushing with all her might. Finally, with a loud thunk, the pear dropped to the ground. The branch flapped powerfully back and forth after being bent

so far downward.

She zoomed toward the fallen fruit, Brenik following right behind her. As she neared the pear, something snatched her mid-air.

"Bat," the voice roared. Bray felt her body being crushed as she looked up into the eyes of a male jovkin. The creature's gold eyes were the same color as Junah's, but only hostility penetrated from his. The horns attached to the sides of his head were large and pointed, and of the two on his forehead, one was broken and half missing.

Bray heard Brenik's voice screeching for help. "Go home, Brenik!" she screamed, hoping he would leave.

He didn't listen and flew up, sinking his teeth into the jovkin's gray hand.

The creature's voice thundered from Brenik's sharp bite, and Bray was slung against the tree. A throbbing pain pulsed through her back and wings before she fell to the ground.

Flying in the air, Brenik circled the jovkin while the creature swiped his hands frantically to snatch him. Bray tried to stand from the ground but crashed back down.

The jovkin watched Brenik closely and seemed to catch on to the routine. Like lightning speeding down from the sky, the creature moved his hand in the other direction to seize Brenik.

Right as the jovkin's hand was about to clasp him, Bray crawled closer and bit the thin, delicate skin of the creature's foot, until blood rippled upward.

Bray glanced wearily up to see Brenik wasn't captured. And just as the jovkin's foot lifted and was about to slam down on top of Bray, another creature dashed from the forest and smashed into their attacker, knocking him backward.

Junah.

Bray sighed in relief as Brenik swooped down beside her, grasping her arms and dragging her with him. "Come on, Bray, help me." His voice was strained.

Bray propped her bare feet flat on the ground, the grass

threading between her toes as she shuffled them toward a wilting tree covered in moss.

Junah was rammed back, but she didn't falter. She lunged forward with incredible speed, her horns aimed at the jovkin's chest and pierced him through his heart.

With all the strength she could muster, Bray stood and watched the male jovkin fall to the ground clasping his chest, ragged breaths escaping his lips.

Junah ran toward them, her eyes filled with dread, and scooped Bray and Brenik up.

"The Pear." Bray reached for the green fruit on the ground.

"Forget it," Brenik said hurriedly.

"No," she demanded. Junah swiped it up before Bray could utter another word and took off running.

"If I had not found you two in time, death would have been unavoidable," Junah snapped.

Brenik did not speak up to say it was Bray's idea to come out to that side of the forest, and she gave him a silent thank you.

"I will let you have the whole pear," she whispered, overcome with guilt for dragging him into trouble.

Brenik shook his head. "No, Bray, I'm fine. You're the one who is hurt—you can have it."

Bray looked up at Junah who had saved them. "We will give it to Junah, then."

Junah shook her head as she hurried the rest of the way through the forest, golden eyes still blazing with fear. "I do not like pears. You two split it."

When Junah finally set them in a lush emerald field, along with the pear, Bray promised herself she would not let Brenik get into trouble again. Bray insisted on Brenik eating more than half the pear, and he did.

Twenty-One

Brenik

Brenik lurched forward on the couch, rubbing at his eyes, trying to erase everything that had happened.

When he had come back from seeing Bray, he stayed on the couch for the remainder of the day and night.

After he finally got up, he went inside the bedroom and found the blood on the floor that he had vomited. Jaw clenched, he slammed the door as hard as he could.

Gripping the sides of his head, he wasn't sure what to do now, but there was his promise to see Bray. So that was what he would do.

If he could have gotten himself drunk without throwing it up, Brenik would have done that—he wanted to forget *everything*. There was no way he could get close to anyone ever again.

It took longer than expected, but he finally arrived at *Wes's* house. Brenik didn't remember exactly how he got there, but somehow, he had. Flattening his hand against the front door, Brenik struck it twice and waited for Bray to answer.

What he really wanted to do was lay on his hammock in the tree hole. Who would have *ever* thought he would think that again, because he sure as hell didn't.

The door swung partially open, and there stood Luca. Even though the kid's hazel eyes were open, Brenik still felt the intensity of his glare.

"I'm not inviting you in," Luca muttered, not budging.

Brenik pushed on the wooden door and stepped inside.

"I guess this isn't like *The Lost Boys*." Luca sighed.

"I never saw it." The movie looked terrible—with annoying kids, like the one in front of him.

"You know, like a vampire can't come in unless they're invited inside?" Luca toed the edge of the doorway, holding his ground.

"I'm not a vampire."

"You have fangs that retract, and you drink blood. You're a vampire."

He ignored the kid's comment, not surprised his sister let everyone know his secret. "Where's Bray?"

"She's in the backyard with Wes. I just came inside to get a drink real quick." Luca brought a Coke can up to his mouth with the tab pulled around and a straw inserted in the hole. He took a long sip as he stared down Brenik.

Who is this kid? He can't drink a soda like a normal person? Brenik shoved past him and headed out the back door. He found Bray standing beside a man with mahogany hair that curled at the ends around his ears and brown skin slightly lighter than Luca's.

As Bray lined up several bricks around the garden, the guy—who must have been Wes—watched her tenderly and affectionately. It made Brenik feel nauseated, reminding him of how he must have looked at Rana.

Wes's head turned to the side and spotted Brenik, his face immediately turning into a scowl.

"Where's Luca?" Wes's voice was low and serious as he approached Brenik. Bray lifted her head and didn't smile either. He guessed that no one was thrilled to see him, even though Bray had wanted him to come.

Brenik couldn't help himself and shrugged. "How should I know?"

Chewing on a granola bar, Luca opened the door just as Wes's expression was getting a bit too intense for Brenik's liking.

"Don't act like a—"

"A what?" Brenik smiled sweetly after interrupting Wes and staring at Luca.

Ignoring Brenik, Wes nodded toward the door. "Luca, can you go back inside for a little while?"

"Why?" Luca whined. Wes narrowed his eyes and the kid must have got the drift. "Fine, I'll go inside."

After Luca shut the door behind him, Bray wandered over to Brenik. "Have you figured anything out?"

"You mean since I murdered Rana? No, I haven't figured out anything besides sulking on the couch." Brenik knew he was being a dick, but he was too miserable to worry about it.

Wes tugged Bray's elbow. "I think he needs to leave, Bray."

"What are you going to do? Call the cops?" Brenik taunted.

Wes moved forward, shoulders pulled back. "Yes."

"You know what? Fuck off. You don't own me, or this house, or that tree. If Ruth could have written me and Bray in a will, this would have been our house." He wasn't going to let some asshole take over everything in his life.

"Bray's welcome to stay as long as she wants." Wes shoved a finger at Brenik's chest. "But you need to leave."

"I can answer for myself," Bray piped in.

Brenik didn't know this *Wes*, and he knew he shouldn't be starting shit, but he couldn't muster the strength to care. His anger lessened as he grew frustrated when he thought about what all had happened. If his mind kept swirling with thoughts of everything he had done, he would collapse to his knees in front of them and never get back up.

"Do you want to eat dinner with us?" Bray asked,

attempting to break the tension.

Brenik was about to explode with that asinine question from Bray. "I. Can't. Eat."

Wincing, Bray spoke quickly, "Right, I'm sorry. Croquet?"

"Is this a joke? I mean, are we serious here, Bray?"

"I don't know. I don't know. I *don't* know!" she screamed.

Brenik had rarely ever seen his sister angry, and he put his hands on her shoulders to stop them from shaking. "Chill, Bray. I'll play a game of croquet."

A sound came from inside the house, and they all turned to a window being shut. Luca had been listening through the small open gap.

Luca came outside, and they all acted as if nothing had even happened as Bray and the kid set up the game to play.

Brenik decided that this was one of the stupidest things he had ever done in his life—playing a game of croquet with these people.

Wes stood too close to Brenik, watching every one of his tiny movements, as if he thought Brenik was going to rip Luca's throat apart. He wouldn't touch the kid's rotten blood with the end of his croquet stick.

Every time the kid got his ball through the hole, Bray would cheer and pat his little black head like he had just done something amazing for humanity. In actuality, all he did was strike a fucking ball.

Anyone here could do it. Well, except for Bray, who continued to struggle with each swing. Wes stood behind her as close as he could, probably to press himself against her.

Brenik couldn't watch the vomit-inducing family show a moment longer. He wanted to head back to the cabin to be alone. Without a goodbye, Brenik set the mallet down and walked out the gate.

Steps crunching through the grass came from behind him. "Bray." He sagged his shoulders and lowered his chin. "I just need to be alone, okay?"

“I’m not Bray.”

Turning around to the sound of Luca’s annoying voice, Brenik let out a sigh. “Listen, kid, I’m going to be truthful here. I don’t feel like talking to you.” He said it as nicely as he possibly could.

“After school, can you come by to finish the game?” Luca asked.

“Who are you? Seriously, *who* are you?”

“Luca, duh.”

“But why do you want me to come back? You know what I am.” Brenik looked down at him with narrowed eyes.

“I know… But I know how much Bray wants to help you.”

His sister rounded the corner at that moment, trailed by Wes. “Leaving already?” she asked.

“Let me go home and think”—he paused and studied Luca—“but I’ll be here tomorrow to finish the game after Luca gets out of school.”

He felt his stomach heave when he thought about school—Rana was Luca’s teacher… *Was.*

Brenik left and moved Rana’s car to a different cabin after he got home. He couldn’t look at it any longer. Eventually someone would report her missing, and he would turn himself in. Holding back another breakdown, Brenik went into the bedroom and scrubbed the blood off the floor, hot tears sliding down his cheeks.

He picked up the dresser and placed it back against the wall. The mirror was broken in fragments strewn across the floor. Before cleaning them up, he glanced at the painting. His heart sped up because that portrait had caused so many things—the bad was conquering all the good. To ease his torment, he picked up a piece of glass and brought it up to his face to inspect it. As his chest sank in, Brenik pushed the glass to the center of his wrist. He pressed down until there was a prickling pain, then he steadily slid the glass across his skin, hoping to leave all his suffering behind.

The flesh opened, but the blood stayed inside, even with the stinging sensation. He slammed the shard of glass against the wall, and watched it shatter into smaller fragments that he wished were himself.

Brenik had an idea when he woke up late the next day. He headed to the library and found a woman with gray hair pulled into a low bun and a face covered in wrinkles. "May I help you?" she asked.

Running a hand through his hair, Brenik thought about what he should say. "Do you have the Dorian Gray book?"

"*The Picture of Dorian Gray*?"

He wasn't sure. "Yes."

"If we do it will be in the fiction section under Wilde," she responded with a lazy tone and a flick of her hand.

"Can you spell that for me?" Brenik asked, attempting to sound it out in his head. He knew from the beginning sound that it started with a *W*.

"W-I-L-D-E," she said slowly and pointed to the aisle straight ahead.

Brenik nodded and walked in the direction of the fiction row where she had directed him. Gritting his teeth at the sentences on the spines he couldn't read, he thought the librarian should have at least offered to help him find the book. Maybe he should have asked her, but he wanted to find it on his own—to prove to himself he could.

Somehow, he passed over the book and was in the section containing authors with *Y* last names, so he scanned his way back and found the dark spine. He couldn't make out the words, but there were five of them—and there were five words in *The Picture of Dorian Gray*, when he ticked them off on his fingers. Quickly tugging the book out, he stuffed it into the back of his pants and shuffled past the librarian.

"Couldn't find it?" she asked, while scanning him up and down.

"I changed my mind on what I want to do my report on. I'll come back when I figure it out, though."

"You could do *Jane Eyre*. That is a lovely one," she suggested.

"Maybe." He shrugged and glanced up at the large clock by the exit door. It was already close to the time school would let out.

Brenik made it to the school within five short minutes. The pickup line was already filled, and he hurried to the front of the building, right as the bell rang.

After a pack of kids rushed out, Luca and his redheaded, freckled friend strolled out, taking their precious time.

Luca lifted his head and noticed Brenik, then lowered his brows in confusion. "I thought you were supposed to come to our house later."

"I'm here to pick you up," Brenik stated, needing the redhead to take a hike.

"You don't have a car." Luca peered out toward the parking lot.

"Stranger danger?" Freckles asked in a whisper. If only the redheaded kid knew what a danger Brenik really was.

"Nah. This is Bray's brother."

"Dude, she is seriously hot." Freckles elbowed Luca's ribs, and Brenik wanted to crack off the kid's arm for talking about his sister.

"Right. Anyway, scurry on now." Brenik motioned with his hand for Freckles to go away.

Freckles gave the kid an icy look, and Luca nodded him on.

"What's going on?" Luca asked after the other kid was gone. Not a single shudder of fear was visible as he waited for Brenik to answer.

"I need your help." Brenik waved him away from the

school, and Luca followed as they started for his cabin.

"Why me? Can't you ask Bray?" Luca challenged when they got to the sidewalk.

"No, she is always stuck on being a savior." Bray had such a good heart, and his was a blackened disaster.

"You do know I'm a kid, right?"

"You do know when I was two I found bodies slaughtered, right?" The kid needed to realize you have to grow up.

Luca's eyes widened with surprise, but not fright. "We're learning about World War II in school right now."

Brenik stopped walking and turned to Luca. "What does that have to do with anything?"

"Kids younger than me had to deal with a lot, so whatever you need, I'll help you face it." *Another savior.* No wonder Luca and Bray got along so well.

"That isn't even relatable."

"It kind of is. Bravery is key."

"Are you a public speaker now?" Before the conversation got into stupid territory, Brenik pulled out the book from the waist of his pants. "Have you read this?"

Luca snatched the book from Brenik's hand and inspected it. "I haven't, but I can scan it over."

"Do you think Bray and Wes are going to get upset if you don't come straight home?" Brenik didn't care what they thought, but he wouldn't force the kid to come.

"Yep. At least I know Wes is going to be pissed." Luca sighed.

"Good." Brenik grinned because Wes seemed like a jackass.

"It shouldn't take me too long to read over the pages. Do you not know how to read?" Luca's eyes seemed to search Brenik's face for an answer.

"I can read letters, but I'm not good with actual books." Brenik was never interested in learning, and even when he tried, it was incredibly hard for him. He now wished he had listened to Ruth and tried harder.

By the time they reached the cabin, Luca had started going over vampire theories. Brenik thought he had made a mistake by bringing the kid with him because the talking never stopped.

Once inside the cabin, Luca went to sit on the couch while Brenik headed to the bedroom to grab his portrait. He brought it into the living room and set it down on the coffee table. "This is what the Stone of Desire gave me. I thought it was what I wanted, but it isn't. Can you help me?"

Twenty-Two

Bray

Bray finished writing several chapters in her spiral notebook, not realizing what time it was. A truck engine pulled into the driveway, signaling Wes's arrival.

She closed the notebook and looked at the time—it was already four o'clock. The front door opened, and Wes walked inside.

"Luca isn't with you?" Bray asked when she noticed he was by himself.

Wes scratched the side of his head. "No. He was supposed to walk home today."

"He hasn't come home yet." Bray grew nervous as she chewed on the inside of her cheek.

"Is your brother here?" Wes asked.

"No, but he didn't give a precise time." He had only said after Luca got out of school.

"Let me call Kyle's house." Wes went into the kitchen and lifted the phone receiver to dial the number.

"Kyle? Hey, it's Wes. Is Luca there with you?" He paused as he listened. "He *what*? Okay, thanks. No, it's not a problem."

Wes hung the phone up and nervously looked at Bray.

"Luca left school with Brenik."

"Why would he do that?" Bray didn't think Brenik would harm him on purpose, but she didn't know if he might unintentionally hurt Luca. *Why wouldn't Brenik just bring Luca to the house?*

"If something happens to him, Bray, I'm going to murder him." Wes gritted his teeth and steam practically radiated off him. Brenik was her brother, but if something happened to Luca, she would strangle him herself.

Twenty-Three

Brenik

"Did you find anything in there?" Brenik asked Luca. The kid was absorbed in the yellowed pages.

"It's a rather dull story, but there *is* a painting. His grows hideous, though, while yours still looks like you." Luca glanced from Brenik's face to the portrait.

"I don't have an answer for that." He wished he did. Brenik paced back and forth, practically digging craters into the floor.

Luca closed the book. "You didn't ask the Stone any of these questions?"

"I don't know, kid. I honestly didn't even care about the staying beautiful forever aspect. All I know is that I didn't want to wither away like Ruth—the woman who took care of Bray and me. I just wanted to be human. That day, I was so overcome with emotion that I wasn't even thinking straight. I didn't know what I wanted. I didn't know what I wanted until I met Rana."

Luca winced when Brenik spoke Rana's name but recovered quickly. "Anyway, in the book, Dorian stabs the portrait and that's what kills him. You aren't going to try that though, are you?"

I just might. A pounding on the door stopped him from pursuing the idea further.

"Wait here," Brenik said.

"I think I'm in trouble," Luca mumbled.

Brenik pulled open the door and Wes stormed in with Bray marching in behind him. "Where is he?" Wes boomed.

"I'm over here, Wes," Luca said. He raised the book in the air, and Wes sighed in relief.

"Brenik, why is he here? Why would you bring him to your cabin?" Bray asked, marching up to Brenik.

He took a step back. "I needed Luca to read something for me."

"I could have read for you," she insisted. He knew his sister would have, but it wasn't something she should concern herself with.

"Not this. You've already helped enough. I needed to figure out a way to end this." Brenik's gaze flicked toward the ceiling.

Bray reached forward and gripped his arm, catching a glimpse of the closed wound from the night before. "Did you do this to yourself?" she gasped.

Ripping his arm out of her grasp, he took several steps back. "It's none of your business."

"It is her business—she's your family. And it's *my* business because you kidnapped my little brother." Wes pointed one too many times at Brenik's chest.

"Hold on. Nobody kidnapped your little brother. He came of his own free will, so you can get the hell out of my house." Brenik sneered.

Wes worked his jaw back and forth. "This isn't even *your* house."

The pent-up rage was boiling inside him, ready to erupt, and he couldn't hold anything back. "Who the hell do you think you are walking in here and into my life like you own everything—like you own my sister? Let me guess, you have her as a pet to fuck because she can't live on her own, so it's *easy* for you."

As soon as he said the words, Brenik knew they weren't true from the way Wes had looked at Bray the other day. Before he could take anything back, a fist collided with his face and he stumbled backward.

The strike stung but it felt good, and he wasn't sorry anymore for saying those words. Brenik brought his hands up and shoved Wes in the chest—both their faces were contorted with ire.

"Brenik, you can't say stuff like that in front of Luca," Bray yelled. But he didn't care. All he cared about was getting this asshole away from him.

Brenik lunged forward and knocked Wes against the sheetrock, striking his face with his closed fist. He pounded him several times while Bray tried to tear him off Wes, but Brenik pushed her to the side.

Wes shoved him back, and Brenik took hold of Wes's shirt. Bray tugged at Brenik's arm again to stop him. With a little too much force, he shoved her back as hard as he could. He needed her to leave him alone for a minute.

A loud crack reverberated in the room and Brenik whirled around, releasing Wes's shirt. When he peered down, he froze—it wasn't Bray he had pushed back, it was Luca. The tiny kid lay on the floor next to the coffee table, knocked out cold. Something about his still body wasn't right. Then Brenik realized it. The kid was dead—blood rested on the edge of the table where his little head had struck.

No one said anything. No one moved an inch, until Bray cried, "No!"

Wes ran forward, nudging Bray to the side as he lifted Luca into his arms and sobbed uncontrollably.

Brenik stood there frozen in pain for what he had done to the small child. A kid he wasn't sure if he even liked, but had developed a slight fondness for. He felt—he felt sickened. *It should have been me instead.*

Bray looked at Brenik. He found no trace of anger on her

face, only genuine hurt as tears rained down her face. "Brenik, why do you have to be so *selfish* all the time? Why do you have to destroy everything that's *good?*" Her voice sounded lost and heartbroken. It reminded him of losing Ruth—it had him thinking about leaving Junah. But most of all, it had him wishing he had never existed.

The decisions he made had been wrong—choices he thought would help himself. He didn't care about himself anymore. Brenik only wanted Bray to be happy, and if he lived a second longer, he would destroy anything good that could happen for her.

Brenik grabbed the portrait from the couch and ran to the kitchen. Despite the anxious pounding of his heart as he ripped open the silverware drawer, there was a contentment there, too. He pulled out the largest knife he could find while holding up the canvas to the light. Without any more hesitation, he didn't just stab the portrait—he hacked at it with fury, with loathing, with hate, with despair, with emptiness, and with love for his sister—who was always his protector. Who he now wanted to protect. Everything about himself he wanted *gone*.

"What are you *doing?*" A shrill voice he thought was Bray's pulsed in his ears. But he felt dizzy and everything was moving in slow motion. His knees buckled beneath him, and he collapsed to the floor.

Harsh agony charged through him, slicing and shredding. He couldn't hold back the scream that tore from his throat. All the cuts he inflicted on the portrait were appearing on him— so much pain—and he wished he didn't deserve it.

Brenik rolled to his back and stilled. A heart-shaped face hovered over his, similar to his own. "I'm sorry. I'm so fucking sorry," he whispered, and his voice cracked on the last word as tears welled in his eyes.

"We'll fix this. I promise we'll fix it," she said in a hushed tone, her hands trying to cover up all the wounds pouring out blood. There was *no way* to fix all the gashes. They were peeling apart, some tearing open all the way to the bone.

"Take him, Bray. Take Luca to the Stone." Brenik pushed the words out.

"And you." She tried to lift his upper body but couldn't.

"No. Just him." He could feel himself already drifting away, coming to the end of his story.

Bray stroked her thumb across his forehead. "I love you, little brother."

"I know." He loved her, too, because she was the better half of him. The last thing he heard was Brayora's mad screams, the last thing he felt was her slapping his chest to live, the last thing he saw was her sorrowful face, and the last thing he wanted was for her to be happy—even if he had already destroyed everything.

Twenty-Four

Bray

Bray hovered over Brenik's still form—his body was covered in bloody gashes as if someone had hacked at his flesh. She wanted to sew the pieces shut, but it was too late. His body began to disintegrate into dirt, the same way Rana's had. Bray let the dirt crumble from her hands and stared up at the painting on the countertop, which had turned into soil, too.

Her body shook as she looked over her shoulder at Wes. He still held Luca's lifeless body in his lap, tears slipping down to his little brother's small face.

What Brenik had said about the Stone of Desire suddenly clicked in her head. "We have to leave now," she said hurriedly. "You will have to drive through the forest quickly."

Tearing his eyes from Luca, Wes asked, "What do you mean?"

"No questions. I'll hold Luca and give you directions from the backseat. You need to get us to the Stone of Desire before it's too late." Bray didn't know if anything could be done, but if it could… She didn't want to hope too much.

Wes still looked as if he wanted to ask questions, but he had Luca in his arms and was already headed for the door. Bray gazed one more time with regret at what remained of Brenik, and for the first time, she left her brother behind.

Bray got into the backseat of the car, and Wes tenderly lay Luca's body in her arms. Blood seeped from the wound, and she wished she could close it somehow—like she wished she could have done for Brenik.

"This is all my fault," Wes cried as he hurled himself into the car.

Bray didn't say anything. It wasn't anyone's fault, just a series of bad choices, and an accident that wasn't meant to have happened.

Holding Luca pressed tightly against her chest, Bray rambled off directions at Wes. He drove as fast as he could through the trees, but not as quickly as they wanted.

"Stop!" Bray yelled, and Wes slammed on the brakes. She could see the Stone's white shape protruding past the bushes.

Throwing open the door, Bray started to lift Luca, but Wes gently took him in his arms.

Bray knew Wes was confused about what she was trying to do, but there wasn't much time, if any at all. She ran for the Stone and placed her hand against the alabaster, rose-shaped top. "Please. Please, answer me this time." There wasn't a response. "Wes, hurry and put your hand on the stone."

Without a word, Wes pressed his hand against the rock and continued to hold Luca in his arms. Bray shook her head frantically at Wes to ask the Stone what he desired, and so he did. "I—I need you to save Luca. He means everything in this world to me, and I can't live without him. Please don't let him die—please bring him back to me." His voice sounded weak and drained, barely making it through his words.

The breaths in Bray's chest came out shakily, and she couldn't find enough air as they waited for something to happen. But nothing did.

"Please! You're the cause of this for what you did to Brenik. So please, make this right!" She slapped at the Stone, full of exasperation.

Under her feet, the chunks of dirt trembled, causing her to stumble backward. With Luca still firmly pressed against his chest, Wes stepped back beside her with fear in his eyes.

Out of the ground, the rest of the pale rock pulled itself up to incredible height, long arms drawing forward.

Black eyes inside a bald white head pushed out of its shell. The creature who she thanked so many times before for helping them, she now wished had never answered her the first time.

Its head didn't come in her direction—it moved toward Wes. "What is it you desire, human?" Although there wasn't a mouth, they both still heard the pounding words inside their skulls.

"My brother… Can you save him?" Wes asked with plea in every single one of those words.

The Stone leaned closer toward Luca, tilting its head, as if sniffing at the small boy's scent. "I can."

Sighing deeply, Wes's shoulders relaxed a little. However, Bray's didn't because she remembered what had happened with Rana. The Stone had said he could save her, too, but she had already been something less than human. Maybe this was different. They had to try.

The Stone's hand dragged toward them, and Bray nudged Wes forward so he could lay Luca's body into the palm of its hand.

Like before with Rana, it closed its fingers around Luca's fragile body. It pulled its hand back to whatever darkness, or light—or combination—could perform the task.

They waited for what seemed like more years than she had lived, until the Stone's hand slowly pushed back out. Each of the fingers blossomed to reveal Luca still lying motionless in the center of the Stone's palm.

Bray's chest sank with disappointment, and a fierce tension built a wall around her. She couldn't look at Wes anymore, who still had hope written all over his face.

"His body was too late to save," the Stone rasped loudly. Even though its voice rumbled inside her head, there was heartache hidden there too.

Crashing to his knees, Wes smacked his hands against his forehead and gripped his hair.

The Stone inched closer. "This was always meant to happen. He will return. When your world is ending"—its head shifted to Bray—"he will be the only one possessing the power to grant passage for mankind into your old world." Was it talking about *Laith*?

"What are you talking about?" Bray demanded. "What do you mean he will return?" She needed direct answers, not the riddled explanations that were never complete.

"You will know."

How will I know?

"When will he come back?" Wes asked. "Where is he now?" Luca still wasn't moving.

"I could not save his body, but I could save his soul. The soul is now split between the two of you. He will be reborn."

Wes seemed unable to grasp or understand what the Stone was saying. He picked up Luca's body and stared at him, begging Luca to wake up.

"What do you mean reborn? When? *How?*" Wes asked, looking down at Luca and then up in the direction of the Stone. But the Stone was already curling back into its natural form, no longer willing to give any more answers.

They watched as the Stone sank back into the ground. All that was left was the large alabaster-colored slab with a rose-shaped top.

"I don't understand." Wes cradled Luca as he moved beside her.

Bray let out a sorrowful sigh. "His soul is split inside me and you."

"I heard that." He may have heard it, but he was still confused. She, however, understood it perfectly.

"He will be reborn, but in order to be reborn, it will have to be between you and me. As in, Luca will be starting over as a baby." She closed her eyes and let the words sink in. Then she flicked them back open to see Wes's horrified face.

"What the hell? So, that thing put half of Luca's soul in my dick, and I have to have sex with you to recreate Luca? How's that even the same thing? He still wouldn't be *him*—he wouldn't even look the same, and you're not even human!" he shouted.

Her stomach dropped at those harsh words, but Wes had every right to say them. This was her fault for bringing Brenik here. This was her fault for wanting to use the gift that the Stone had given her. This was her fault for getting close to these two humans, and this was her fault for not trying to help Brenik more. She had never hated herself before, but at that moment she did.

"I know, it's all my fault," she murmured. She wouldn't say sorry, because sorry couldn't even begin to fix what had happened.

Without one more look at the little beast, or Wes—who made her feel something more than unworthy—Bray changed forms and hurried through the air to get back to her tree, where she would stay to suffer.

The tree was still a disaster inside from Brenik's earlier desperation, and Bray chose to leave it that way. Day after day, she slept on the floor and would only come out to eat.

Eventually, she decided she was going to find somewhere else to live. It felt as if months had gone by, but it had only been ten days.

Wes hadn't spoken to her, but she had heard the engine of his work truck or car when he would leave to go somewhere.

Rolling to her back on the floor, Bray stared up at her and Brenik's words on the ceiling. Each day she had carved a new word into the wood: *selfish, lost, hate, missed, broken, insanity, misunderstood, heart, longing,* and *Hook.*

The sound of the back gate opening and closing radiated into the tree, but Bray didn't move. Even when the branches groaned and the vibrations could be felt through her wooden cell, she stayed perfectly still.

Bray turned to her side away from the hole. She didn't want to see Wes.

Something poked her back, and she turned around to find a large folded piece of paper. She looked toward the outside and didn't see anyone there.

She wanted to throw the paper back out of the hole, but she was curious. With shaky fingers, she unfolded the note to messy handwriting written in black ink.

Bray,
I'm sorry for what I said. I didn't mean it. Please meet me outside because I'll piss my pants if I have to wait up here in the tree for another second.

Wes

Bray didn't rush to meet him outside—she made him wait a couple of minutes. Slowly, she walked to the opening, and peered out to see Wes tightly gripping the branch above. She frowned and crossed her arms. "How long would you have waited?"

"An eternity," he said softly, eyes locked on hers.

"We both know that's a lie."

Trembling, Wes edged closer to where she was. "I was remembering when I carried you into the dollar store and you said, 'this isn't *Pretty Woman*.' Since this is your apartment in a way, I wanted to climb up like the guy scales the stairs in the end.”

The words hit her heart, but then she remembered the rest of the movie. “I’m not a prostitute, either.”

“I know, Bray,” he whispered, looking exhausted. “And I know you’re not a pet or completely human, but you’re special, and I’m sorry. I’m not going to say I won’t say anything stupid ever again, because we both know I probably will. My mouth can get out of control. Whatever harsh things may come out when we argue, we both know those words aren’t true.”

“I forgive you.” Bray wasn’t good at holding grudges, and she didn’t want to. Especially after all they had lost.

“Now, will you please come down and go inside?” His body wavered, and he looked as if he might throw up.

“You want me to go inside the house?”

“Please.”

In her own way, she answered Wes by flying past him and waiting for him at the door. She watched as he climbed unsteadily down the tree, then headed for the house. He opened the door, and she flew straight to the couch and shifted forms.

“I’m so sorry, Wes,” she finally said gently. There wasn’t much else she could say.

Wes let out a long sigh. “I had time to think, time to hate, time to think some more. It was everyone’s fault, and it was no one’s fault. But you lost a brother, too. Not just me.”

It was as though she had lost two brothers, and if she said that out loud, the feeling would cause her to break down. And she might never stop. “What happened afterward?”

Wes leaned against the couch and propped his head on the back of it, rubbing his tired eyes. “I went to the hospital, and it was a big mess. I had to do a whole lot of lying mixed with some truth, and say this guy posed as a family member and kidnapped Luca. The police went to the cabin and since his body is now dirt, which I couldn’t say, they are still after him.

He's also wanted for Rana Alvi's kidnapping.

"I had to tell Kyle not to bring up your name because you were out of town for a few weeks, and Luca wouldn't want you to be a part of this mess. I shouldn't have asked that of him, but he seemed to understand, so he just told the police how this strange guy came to the school twice."

Bray didn't know what to think or feel. She had spent so much time in the tree crying because she wanted both boys there—her little brother and her little beast. She knew she could only get one back.

Tears beaded on Wes's lower lashes, and she reached over to wipe them away. "Do you want to bring him back?" she asked quietly.

Wes's body stilled. "I know what you're getting at, and I'm not going to force you into that. It's also way too soon to think about babies. You have your whole life ahead of you. Somehow, we'll tell people you have amnesia, get you a social security card, and then you can go to school or work or whatever. Not just sit in the house or a tree for the rest of your life."

"I can still do all that, but I want to bring him back." Bray couldn't imagine a world without Luca in it.

"I told you, it's not the same thing," he said, his voice on the verge of breaking.

"I'm not human, remember, so this is an unusual circumstance. I may not get pregnant the first time, either."

Bray couldn't stop all the tears that started to slide down Wes's cheeks, and she mirrored him with the same wet streaks on hers. She hitched her leg around his waist to sit in his lap. Bringing her face close to Wes's, she stroked her nose gently against his, and he closed his eyes.

Wes's lips were slightly parted, and Bray brushed her mouth against his with a soft touch, before pulling back calm and steady. His eyelids shot open and warm brown eyes stared into hers adoringly. Bray's gaze fell to the pale scar above his lip, and she leaned forward to kiss it.

She lifted Wes's shirt over his head and ran her hands up his back. He reached around and pulled out the rubber band at the end of her braid, before slowly unraveling her hair.

He entangled his fingers in her free locks and stared at her with longing. "Do you want me to sing for you?"

"What?" She grinned at the strange question.

"We've danced together—I figured we might as well try everything. So, why not serenade you." Wes shrugged. Then he started to sing, terribly, but better than her, as he stroked his hand across her lower back. A small smile tugged at his lips as his eyes filled with tears. Even though she loved the original song by 10,000 Maniacs, she liked his version better.

Bray smiled, laughing softly as she drew her dress over her head with more tears flowing down her cheeks. She wrapped her arms around Wes, his head falling in between her breasts, and he sobbed.

Her body convulsed from her own weeping as she held him, skin pressed against skin. She knew it was too soon to have a baby, but if there was a way to get one of the boys back, she would do it—not only for herself but for Wes. For Luca.

Unwrapping her arms from around him, Bray tilted Wes's chin up to look at her. "We'll get Luca back."

Reaching forward, Wes placed his palm to her chest. "This is what makes you beautiful, Bray… Your heart." Her chest swelled at his words, his touch. He leaned forward and kissed the delicate area and caressed his way up, until he met her mouth.

Bray brought her hands up and ran them through his hair, lifting herself a little so he could slide his pants down. As their clothes came off, everything became muted—at that moment only the two of them existed in the world.

His lips molded and glided sweetly along with hers. He nipped at her lip, her shoulder, her breast. Then Wes's mouth found hers again, and she lowered herself down on him, both gasping in pleasure as he filled her.

Wes's fingers gripped her hips and rocked her back and forth. As she moved in slow circles, warmth stirred within her. Neither one of them closed their eyes as they watched each other with something developing between them, a seed of emotion that was continuing to grow.

Her pace picked up, his fingers digging in harder, and they got lost in each other, the moment, until the warmth within her ignited into something new, fiery, beautiful. Burning brightly. She gasped, he groaned, both finding the relief and escape they needed.

Bray crashed against Wes's chest, and he held her tight. No longer drowning at that moment, but flying higher than the kite that was in the park the day when it was Wes, Bray, and Luca. She pretended for a moment they were all back at the park watching the kite, and Brenik was there standing beside them with a gentle smile on his face.

Epilogue

Luca
Twenty-Six Years Later

Luca remembered everything as he grew in Bray's womb. He had taken on traits from both Wes and Bray, and because Bray's kind knew everything from the time of conception, so had he. Except he remembered his past life as well.

It had been strange for him to start all over, and although biologically they were his parents, they remained Wes and Bray to him.

He never understood what he was meant to do when Bray and Wes had told him what the Stone of Desire had prophesied. And as years went by, he had thought the Stone must have been mistaken about him.

When it came to Brenik, Luca never blamed him for what had happened. He was more upset that he didn't find a way to save him. In the end, he knew Brenik was happier that he didn't have to live another day with what he had turned into.

But Luca knew what he had to do now. His world was being destroyed: wars were tearing people apart and natural disasters were quickly destroying Earth.

He had gathered as many people as he could—those who

believed him—and they were going to cross into Laith. The place where Bray had run from and where she would be returning to after all these years.

Bray peered up at Luca with her bright blue eyes, matching the ones he'd inherited from her. The permanent crease between her brows only deepened as she studied the crowd. Even at forty-six, she was still beautiful.

"We're with you every step of the way," she said to Luca as she squeezed Wes's hand.

Wes gripped Luca's shoulder like he was afraid Luca would disappear, but he finally released him.

Heart pounding in his chest, Luca walked toward the rose-shaped rock and placed his hand on top. Everyone behind them watched on in silence.

Closing his eyes, he spoke to the Stone. "We're ready to leave this world and escape to the next to save however many lives we can."

Luca's wife brushed his fingers with hers while holding their six-month-old daughter propped on her hip, as they waited for the Stone to answer.

Did you enjoy Clouded By Envy?
Authors always appreciate reviews, whether long or short.

Want more Cruel Curses? Check out Veiled By Desire, Book Two, in the Cruel Curses series!

Sometimes fate has other plans…

In Laith, when the moons are high, Tavarra gains the ability to walk the land, losing her seahorse-like tail. But should she remain out of the water, a curse will consume her, turning her into a beast with sharp fangs and long claws. A creature that, on some nights, becomes a rampaging monster.

Rhona and her village are under a sinister leader's control. He took Rhona from the man she loves, stripped away her water ability, then forces her to retrieve a coveted prism that will increase his powers.

When Tavarra and Rhona cross paths, they agree to help each other succeed. They then embark on separate missions in hopes of breaking Tavarra's curse and saving Rhona's loved ones. But with an untamable beast inside Tavarra, and Rhona having to wander through a dangerous forest with a man who sparks her desire, nothing is certain...

Subscribe to Candace's Awesome Newsletter for the latest news and giveaways!

Join Candace's Facebook Group: Candace's Pretty Monsters

Also From Candace Robinson

Wicked Souls Duology
Vault of Glass
Bride of Glass

Marked by Magic Duology
The Bone Valley
Merciless Stars

Cruel Curses Trilogy
Clouded By Envy
Veiled By Desire
Shadowed By Despair

Faeries of Oz Series
Lion (Short Story Prequel)
Tin
Crow
Ozma
Tik-Tok

Cursed Hearts Duology
Lyrics & Curses
Music & Mirrors

Immortal Letters Duology
Dearest Clementine: Dark and Romantic Monstrous Tales
Dearest Dorin: A Romantic Ghostly Tale

Campfire Fantasy Tales Series
Lullaby of Flames
A Layer Hidden
The Celebration Game
Mirror, Mirror

These Vicious Thorns: Tales of the Lovely Grim
Between the Quiet
Hearts Are Like Balloons
Bacon Pie
Avocado Bliss

Vampires in Wonderland Series
Rav (Short Story Prequel)
Maddie
Chess
Knave

Acknowledgments

To the readers, thank you for coming on the journey with Brenik and Bray. These two characters are ones who will stay with me forever, especially Brenik.

I'd like to also thank the people who helped me make this book better when it was still not quite there yet, Danielle Smoot, Gerardo Delgadillo, and Donna Weiss. A special thanks to Patricia Thibodeaux, Kattie Sivley and Luke Taylor for reading this early and giving me your awesome opinions.

Live Knudsen, you were super lovely to work with, and I appreciate all your encouragement in the manuscript comments as you helped me build onto this book. Jackie, you were wonderful as too! Hannah, the cover you created is exactly what I envisioned!

As always, my husband, Nathan, my daughter, Arwen—I love you both. Mom, you're always there for me when I need it. Victoria Robinson, you have been with me on this writing journey since day one, and you continue to read each book early—sometimes multiple times.

This story wouldn't have come to life without my love for the 90s, fantasy, vampires, bats, and Dorian Gray—a combination that I would love to be a part of.

About the Author

Candace Robinson spends her days consumed by words and hoping to one day find her own DeLorean time machine. Her life consists of avoiding migraines, admiring Bonsai trees, watching classic movies, and living with her husband and daughter in Texas—where it can be forty degrees one day and eighty the next.

Connect with Candace:

Website: https://authorcandacerobinson.wordpress.com/
Facebook: https://www.facebook.com/literarydust
Twitter: https://twitter.com/literarydust
Instagram:
https://www.instagram.com/candacerobinsonbooks/
Goodreads:
https://www.goodreads.com/author/show/16541001.Candace
_Robinson or ignore that and just try searching for Candace Robinson!

www.ingramcontent.com/pod-product-compliance
Lightning Source LLC
Chambersburg PA
CBHW051222210726
48290CB00003B/745